KAYLA WREN

Their Mountain Captive

BLACK CHERRY
PUBLISHING

Contents

Keep in touch with Kayla!

Want to hear about new releases, sales, bonus content and other cool stuff? Sign up for Kayla's newsletter at www.kaylawrenauthor.com/newsletter!

1

Roxy

The mountains are cold. Even with golden sunshine filtering through the branches, the breeze slices straight through my sweatshirt. No one mentioned this on the blog posts I read—that the longer you stay up in the mountains, the more you get chilled to the bone.

The air is thinner, too. For the first few days here, I kept gasping for breath, trying to figure out what was wrong with me.

Well... it's up for debate. But the air thing, that's all on the mountains.

I lift my camera to my eye, fiddling with the focus. Through the lens, miles of craggy pale rock stretch down and away, bristling with trees and shrubs and the odd cabin. The sky yawns wide open overhead, so close I could almost touch it, and *yes*.

This is perfect. This will take my travel blog to the next level. "Suck it, *Travels with Jenny*."

I started talking to myself on the third day of hiking. I'm a city girl down to my pedicured toes, no matter that they're squashed and blistered now in my boots. I'm so used to having constant bustle around me; to hearing neighbors fight and traffic rumble past in the street. The silence out here, broken only by the whistling breeze and the rushing river and the cries of wildlife...

It's creepy. I can't wait to hear the blare of car horns again.

First, though, I need to document this trip. Create the best damn article I can about solo treks on Lonely Mountain.

This will work. It has to. Because if my blog doesn't work out, if I have to resign myself to a life tapping away in a plain gray cubicle...

Cold sweat breaks out on my spine.

Not gonna happen.

"Come to mama." A squirrel pauses part way up a tree trunk, its fluffy tail twitching as I step closer. It cocks its head, practically posing for the camera, and I grin as I snap a series of photos. "Hell yeah. This is what I'm talking about."

The squirrel twitches its nose.

"Don't judge me," I grumble. "It's freaking lonely out here."

I snap two more photos before the squirrel bounds away up the tree, claws scrabbling against the bark. When I watch it go, my neck aches from tilting my head back so far—these trees don't mess around. All around, they tower into the sky, dwarfing me, reminding me how tiny and soft and fragile I am.

I bite my tongue and snap another photo of the sky, the branches reaching out towards each other like spindly fingers.

A huffed breath makes me freeze. My body's reaction is immediate, instinctual, my muscles tensing as my heart slams in my chest. My brain takes a second longer to catch up, but as I turn, dread is already sliding through my gut.

The bear is twenty feet away. Watching me from between

two trees, its dark fur puffed and bristling. Those eyes are fixed on me, unmoving, its jaw dropping open, and my scream traps in my throat. Comes out as a squeak.

The bear lifts its head and *bellows.* Roars so loud, the stone practically trembles beneath my feet. And I'm stumbling back, ready to run, all those bear safety tips I read before I came wiped clean from my mind, and—

Air whooshes past me. I'm weightless, plummeting, my arms flailing out to the sides—

Crack.

The breath knocks out of me, pain flooding in to take its place. I stare up at the clouds drifting lazily above the branches, too numb to understand.

Shadows creep along the edges of my vision.

I blink.

The world goes dark.

* * *

"Motherfucker!"

The word comes out garbled, the syllables slurring together. I blink hard, my vision fuzzy, the rest of my senses slowly fading back in.

The breeze rustling the trees.

Whooping bird cries.

The lumpy ground beneath my body.

The *pain.* The motherfucking pain.

"Ow ow ow ow ow ow." Tears slide down my cheeks into my hair as I work my way down my body parts. Wiggling fingers; twitching toes. That's what you do, right? Check everything is still working, and not gnawed off by a bear?

3

The bear.

I lurch onto my elbows, cursing roundly at the hot flare of pain in my side. The mountains spin around me then settle, cool and quiet and empty as they were before.

Honestly. That fleabag didn't even have the decency to finish me off. And now I'm stretched out on the rocks, battered and bruised, too woozy to think straight.

I take stock of my surroundings. Breathe slowly, counting to ten as I do. Anything to keep my mind present, to force myself to concentrate.

I've fallen about fifteen feet. Shit, is that all? It felt more like fifty. My backpack is upside down beside the rock face; my poor camera lies within reach.

Smashed. Ruined. I look away, fresh tears stinging my eyes.

Stupid bear. Should be made into a rug.

"Sweet Jesus, that hurts." I tip gingerly over to one side, working my way onto my knees. I pause for a second, my head hanging as dizziness washes over me, then wobble to my feet.

"Mother—"

Okay, not the left foot. Gotcha. I sniffle, peering down the length of my bare leg below my shorts, but other than bruises and scrapes, it doesn't seem mangled. There are no shards of bone or other horror-movie injuries. Just a hot throb of pain when I try to step on that ankle.

"This had better make a good freaking blog post." I'm rambling, not making sense, half delirious with pain as I limp to my camera. I gather up the biggest shards—god knows why—then blink at my backpack.

It seems fine, just tossed around. And there's important stuff in there. Stuff I need to *survive.*

4

But my brain clearly isn't back online yet, because the thought of lifting that weight onto my bruised body...

I can't do it.

"Nope. Sorry," I croak, limping away, my ruined camera clutched in my palms. "Not today. No, thank you."

Lonely Mountain. Freaking Lonely Mountain. I curse this wretched pile of rock for the next twenty minutes, winding my wobbly way to find a path. And when I do, I'm too exhausted and sore to celebrate, limping grimly forward onto the level dirt path, coated in a fine layer of pine needles.

People. I need people. Preferably sane ones and not serial killers. Someone with a phone and a first aid kit; someone who can make this nightmare be *over* already. I try calling out a few times, but my reedy voice bounces through the tree trunks and no one shouts back.

I'm alone. Hurt and lost on the mountain.

And I ditched my backpack.

Fresh tears brim in my eyes.

Nope. Oh, no you don't. I lecture myself sternly, sniffing hard and picking up the pace. This is no time to fall apart. I can do that later, sure, but for now, I need to keep it together. I need to survive this stupid trip to hell, then write a scathing blog post about Lonely Mountain warning everyone else to stay away.

At first, I think the cabin is a mirage. That I'm hallucinating the sturdy wooden structure nestled between the trees. It blends so well to the surroundings, it's practically camouflaged, but it's big, I realize. Not just an outhouse—someone's lodge. With a deck wrapping around the outside, and a stack of chopped firewood tucked under the shelter of the slanted roof.

"Oh my god." I change direction, limping off the path with jerky movements. Making a beeline for safety. The cabin's

5

curtains are drawn, the windows dark, but that *firewood…*

Someone lives here.

The tang of old woodsmoke clings to the cabin. The wooden steps up to the deck groan under my boots, and I grit my teeth against my body's loud complaints. I shouldn't be moving right now—I should be tucked up somewhere warm and sleeping. I should be drifting on clouds of painkillers, or sweetly digesting in the belly of the bear—anything but dragging my sorry ass up these steps. When I reach the top, I might as well have climbed Everest.

I tip my head back and let out a ragged sigh.

Okay. Okay. Just a few more steps. I shuffle across the deck, the wooden boards swept clean of pine needles. A bird startles nearby, exploding out of a tree in a whirl of feathers, but I don't even glance over.

Nearly there.

Tap… tap…

My knock is feeble. I can't get my freaking arm to work. I scowl and knock harder, using every last ounce of my concentration to do it.

Then I wait.

The cabin is silent.

I tip my forehead against the door.

"Come on," I mutter, knocking again. "Don't do this to me, you bastard." Whoever owns this cabin—they'd better get their ass here right this second. Or they'll find a passed out travel blogger on their deck.

Nothing. Silence. I might as well be knocking on a tree. I groan, shaking my head from side to side, my forehead still pressed against the door.

A thought slinks through my mind.

A *bad* thought.

The kind of thought that could get me in trouble.

People who live in the mountains—they're pretty weird, right? Hunters and preppers and loners—Lonely Mountain is famous for drawing the people who don't fit in anywhere else.

Those kinds of people are intense about property. They shoot first and ask questions later, and yet...

Pain throbs sharp in my side.

And yet this is it. My best chance for a rescue.

"Please don't be a nutjob," I pray, reaching down to try the handle. The door's locked, but that's no surprise. What *is* surprising is the surge of energy that crackles through me now I have a plan.

I place the shattered remains of my camera gently on the deck, white spots floating in my eyes as I bend over.

Then I limp back down the wooden steps and hunt around in the undergrowth for a rock.

It doesn't take long. I heft it in my palm as I wobble back to the cabin. I grit my teeth as I climb the steps, barely wincing this time—I'm on a mission.

Door or window?

I've never done this before. How do you break into a cabin? What's the most effective way to get into a building when your body doesn't work, and you don't want the owner to be pissed off at you?

I slam my rock at the door just below the handle. It rattles in the frame. That's it.

Yeah, there's only one way I'm getting in. I limp back a few paces, line up with the window, wind my arm back...

And let fly.

2

Dante

My boots are silent, creeping through the trees, the thick soles cushioned by dried pine needles. I've been here for almost two years and never had a day's trouble, but still the habit stays.

I will never be safe. Not really. Not as long as my brother suspects I am alive. So I move through the mountains on silent feet; I keep to myself and rarely go into town.

I live the life of a paranoid recluse.

It's fine. It's better than the way I lived before.

I was never one for the wilderness before I fled my family's city. I grew up in luxury, surrounded by fine art and fast cars, dressed in tailored clothes.

My flannel shirt shifts over my shoulders.

Things have changed.

When I first came here, broken and alone, I thought Lonely Mountain was ugly. The scarred heap of rock seemed to deserve its name, and the biting wind set my teeth on edge. Even the bird calls grated on my ears, and I questioned my sanity hundreds of times.

I mean, come on. Could I not have started over on a nice tropical island?

This is better, though. My family would never think to look for me here, where luxury is a dirty word. And they underestimate me, because I would give anything—would live in the lowest squalor—to be free of them.

Cold and bored, yes, but free.

The shadows shift around me as I walk, the evening light tinted pink. It's beautiful, in a harsh way. I can see that now. Just like I can name the plants tickling my pant legs; can identify the birds by their calls.

Alec helped me with those things.

Another thing my family would never expect.

The clutch of dead rabbits swings from my hand, and I strain to listen as I walk. They weren't messy deaths—I'm not cruel like the other Marinos—but the scent of blood could still bring bears. There's a gun strapped to my back, more for people than animals, but I'll use it if I have to.

I'll do *anything* if the need is dire enough.

My family taught me that.

It's a relief when I catch the first glimpse of my cabin: a sliver of wood through the dark trees. I'd never admit it to Alec, but when I go out on hikes, I'm never one hundred percent certain I'll find my way back. The mountain is too winding and warren-like; the pale rock face like the moon. But I've never had to call him for help yet, so that's something.

A small victory.

"Grazie Dio." I pick up the pace, the rabbits swinging wider now. I'm too eager to splash water on my cheeks, to grab a beer from the cooler, and I get sloppy.

There's no excuse.

"Dante." A hand snakes out between the trees and grips my forearm. I spin, my hand already on my gun, but it's Alec. Shit.

It's Alec.

His pale, clean-shaven face is grim, his green eyes hard. The back of his hand is laced with old scars, and they stand out white against his knuckles where he grips me.

"Do you want to die?" I hiss, my heart thundering beneath my coarse shirt. I force my stiff fingers to let go of my gun. "Do you want me to shoot your stupid face off?"

"Look at your cabin." He's ignoring me, as always. He's too calm, too unflappable for my outbursts to sink in. My furious words land on Alec's broad shoulders and slide right off, pattering onto the dead leaves.

I tear my scowl away from the other man and peer through the evening gloom. The cabin is still a distance away, blending eerily with the trees, and it takes a minute for me to see what he means.

There.

A darker patch on one window. A gaping hole where there should be glass.

"Motherfucker," I growl.

There's someone in my cabin.

"I passed by at noon. The window was fine." Alec is still holding my forearm. I should shake him off, should storm through the trees and get this shit show over with, but his steady voice reins me in.

"My brother?" I grit the words out. There's only one person still hunting me. I keep tabs on the Marinos—not just through the papers, but through their emails. Their phone lines. Every person in my family believes that I'm dead... except for my younger brother Angelo.

Alec hums. "It's sloppy. Could be a hiker. Or a bear."

I scoff, shaking him off this time. I don't have time for bullshit. There's someone *in my home*. "And this bear picked *my* cabin? Out of all of Lonely Mountain? Doesn't that seem like a fucking coincidence?"

"Dante," Alec calls, but I'm already striding away. Weaving through the trees, breathing hard as I go. The rabbits swing in my hand, not important anymore, but hey—if it is a bear, they'll make a good distraction.

Something tells me a bear wouldn't smash a window. That it would break the goddamn door down, like it was crumpling cardboard.

Alec is right, though. Angelo wouldn't smash a window. He'd case the cabin, surveying it for weeks. He'd tap my phone and steal my food, driving me out of my mind with suspicion and fear. And when he was finally ready to give me a heart attack, he'd leave his calling card.

A black business card, embossed with silver.

Angelo Marino sends his regards.

Grown men have pissed their pants when they found Angelo's card on their doorstep. There's no way he'd miss the chance to do that to me. And when I get close enough, I pause in the shadows, scanning the deck for a black business card.

Nothing. Just glittering shards of glass.

So who the fuck is in my cabin?

"I did a lap before you came." Alec's at my shoulder with no warning, no snapping of twigs. He's better at the mountain life than me—a natural. He moves through the rocky landscape like a ghost. I glance at him, the evening light playing golden in the strands of his tawny hair, and nod.

11

If he says he checked it out, I trust him.

And that's the biggest irony of it all, but I don't have time to stand here and wonder.

My window is smashed.

My home has been breached.

And someone must pay. You can take the Marino out of the mob…

"The front door?" I murmur. It could be a trap. There could be dozens of my father's men inside, bristling with guns and tailored suits. But Alec nods.

"It's the best entry point." I begin to walk forward, but his grip snags my wrist. "Dante. I'll go first."

Fuck. That.

"Absolutely not," I hiss, wrenching my arm away for the second time today. If he thinks I'm going to let him risk his life for me—the only true friend I've ever had—

"Dante." He sounds tired. "I'm trained for this. Remember?"

I don't care. Alec doesn't do that shit anymore—he got a clean slate, same as me. So I don't care that he's probably right, that it's the smart way to do this.

No one cleans up my messes for me.

"Stay out of sight." I stride away before he can argue, ignoring the soft stream of curses I leave behind. I should be careful about this, should do this delicately, but Alec pissed me off with that stupid suggestion.

I've always been hotheaded. No reason that would change along with everything else. So I pound up my deck steps, not even trying to be quiet, and kick open my door.

* * *

A shriek pierces the air of my cabin. Across the room, a young woman sits frozen in horror on my sofa, her dark hair tangled around her shoulders. Her knuckles are white where they grip the seat cushion, and one foot is propped up on my coffee table.

Alec made me that coffee table. He hand-carved the patterns in the wood.

"Who the fuck are you?"

My question is quiet. Deadly. But the door slams shut behind me, and glass crackles under my boots. I stride into the dim interior of my cabin, a thousand possibilities tangling in my head.

Angelo sent her.

It's a hit job.

She's a spy.

She's the dumbest goddamn hiker on these mountains, breaking into a cabin and lounging on the sofa.

"I'll count to five." Her face is ashen as she scrambles to her feet, her boot thumping against my rug. She winces, yes, and that could be convincing—

If Angelo didn't pull this kind of shit all the time.

He loves mind games. Lulling people into a false sense of security, then knocking the legs out from under them. So I pull my gun as I walk forward, heart hardening to stone.

Counting: "One. Two. Three. Four—"

"Stop! Oh my god, stop." She holds up her palms, her hands trembling. And I swear I hear her mutter, *"Prepper freaks."* But then she speaks louder, clearer, her voice surprisingly strong considering the way she's shaking like a leaf.

"I'm Roxy. Roxy Williams. I got hurt hiking, and I came here for help." She talks quickly, edging around the side of the coffee table. Giving herself a clear run at the door. Smart girl. "I'm

13

s-sorry about the window. I'll pay for the damage, I swear."

"Don't move."

She freezes, eyes darting at the doorway. Trying to judge whether she could make it, even though she'd have to go past me.

"Don't try it," I tell her softly. "I won't pause."

I can see the exact moment the truth of that statement sinks in. She sags, her shoulders slumping, her hip still propped over one leg.

Is it true? Could this all be the world's worst luck? Hope blooms in my chest. I could let her go. We could even drop her in town with the mountain rescue, get her some first aid.

"Listen. Listen. Dante, right?" I freeze, my palm growing slick around my gun. She babbles on, not noticing the way the temperature has plummeted. Ice crystals might as well form in my breath. "This isn't a big deal. I'll pay for everything, and—and I'll get out of your way. Right now. Right this minute. I hit my head earlier and I wasn't thinking straight—"

She's shuffling toward the doorway again. I level the gun at her chest.

"How do you know my name, little girl?"

She splutters, wide eyes fixed on the gun. Two spots of color burn high on her pale cheeks, and she actually sounds offended when she speaks.

"*Little*—excuse me? I am a grown woman, you asshole." I twitch the gun and she swallows. Talks faster. "I looked through your drawers. I wasn't stealing, I swear, I was just looking for a phone or—or *anything*. Something to get me out of this mess." She trails off, muttering under her breath, but I've heard enough.

She knows who I am.

14

Alec will know. That's the first thought in my head, and it makes a hard knot sink through my gut. Alec will know that she was here—what I did with her.

"I'm sorry." I even mean it as I raise the gun.

"Dante!" The door swings open behind me. And Alec is here, forcing my outstretched arm down. He murmurs to me like he's trying to calm a spooked horse, his words steady and soothing in my ear. "Don't do that. Not yet. Let's think this through, alright?"

As if Alec would let me kill a girl *after* we talk about it. Bullshit. My chance is gone.

And with it, every last hope I had of a normal life here—that's gone, too.

My ribs are knit tight with loathing as I turn to the woman.

"Do you know what you've fucking done?" I spit the question, and she shakes her head fast, glancing at Alec for help, but she won't find any there.

He has no stomach for killing. But he won't let her just walk out the door either. Not until we think this through, not until we have a *plan.*

"Get on the bed." Alec says, resigned.

Her face goes chalky white. It's a death pallor, and I swallow down a bitter laugh.

"We don't want to touch you, little thief." I twitch the gun toward the bed. "We just want to keep an eye on you."

She eyes me doubtfully, but what can she do? And that realization firms her mouth in a line.

She limps all the way to the bed. She's either an excellent actress, or she really is hurt. I glance at Alec, and he's already nodding. He'll see to her.

What a mess.

15

"This is definitely illegal," she's saying as Alec ties her wrists to the bed frame. Her boots are tramping dirt on my clean sheets. "This is kidnapping, or abduction, or something like that. Are you listening? It's a crime."

"So is breaking and entering," Alec sighs.

He'd know. He may have turned in his badge and his gun, but Alec worked for the FBI for a decade before he quit. Before he tracked me out here, ready to finish things once and for all...

Then showed mercy.

God knows I didn't deserve it.

"What are you going to do with me? It's just a stupid window. What is *wrong* with you two—"

"We're going to treat your cuts. Bind your ankle. Feed you dinner. And go from there, alright?" The way he says it is so reasonable. Like we're doing her a favor, and I stifle a smirk as she blinks, bemused. Then reality sets back in and she scowls, opening her mouth to yell, and Alec slips a gag neatly between her teeth.

"You do that way too easily," I murmur. I can't help myself when it comes to Alec. Nudging him, riling him up—it's my greatest pleasure out here. "Is there something I should know?"

But the smirk slides off my face when Alec stands and turns to me. He is not amused. This isn't funny. And doubt clouds his green eyes.

He's not sure if he's doing the right thing; not sure I'm worth it.

I swallow hard.

"I'll get some supplies," Alec mutters, his gaze dropping to the rug. Then he strides past, and leaves me in the ringing silence.

3

Alec

I make a dozen lists before I even reach my cabin half a mile
away. Some things keep coming back, throbbing between
my temples with their urgency.

We need to treat her injuries.

We need to figure out if Angelo sent her.

We need to find out who she is.

In fact… where the hell is her stuff? No one goes hiking on
Lonely Mountain with nothing but the clothes on their back.
No one without a death wish, anyway, and judging from her
outraged squawk as I slipped the gag into her mouth, this girl
definitely wants to live.

It's not looking good. If Angelo Marino is here somewhere,
biding his time in the trees…

I pick up my pace, striding faster between the rocks, a first
aid kit and other supplies bundled high in my arms.

How the fuck did I get here?

That's the biggest question of all. But I push it away, because I
don't have time for that right now. Don't have time to consider
what kind of FBI agent walks away from his whole life and

17

winds up friends with the man he once hunted.

A really shit one, my brain supplies.

Yeah. Right.

I huff out a breath, walking faster. When I left ten minutes ago, she was tied and gagged and Dante stood nearby. For a horrible, guilt-drenched second I wonder if I should have left at all. If Dante freaked, if he went back to his original plan. And shit, he still has his gun—

My boots thud up the wooden steps just as Dante lets out a yell. I barge through the door, dropping the supplies, arms raised wide, and Dante turns to me.

"Have you seen this shit?"

He's standing over the girl, the cuffs of his plaid shirt perfectly rolled, like he can't quite forget his previous life's tailoring. Despite his yell, he's calm for once, his gray eyes steady and his dark hair smoothed back. Dante has always been like this—thrown into a tantrum by the smallest inconvenience, but cold and calculating in a real tight spot. She glares up at him, pure loathing shining from her eyes, as Dante waves one boot by the heel.

Her leg is stretched out on the bed, the ankle swollen and flushed purple.

"That is grotesque." Dante tosses her boot to the floor, wrinkling his nose. "That looks like something from the deli counter. Alec, she really is injured."

Her eye roll is so exaggerated, her gag shifts on her face. And I want to point out that he just said my name in front of her, that he identified me too, but who am I kidding?

We're in this together.

"Guess she's not a liar." I bend and pick up the supplies one by one. Dante watches me, not helping. "Only a vandal."

18

There's an angry growl behind the gag. Dante snorts, nudging her elbow with his knee.

"Don't get pissy, little girl. You don't want to be called a vandal? Don't break a man's window."

I don't point out that we've committed easily the worst crime today. Dante knows.

"We need to find out who she is."

"Roxy Williams," Dante supplies immediately. He frowns down at her. "That's the name she gave, anyway."

"Her license?"

For the first time, Dante notices her lack of *stuff*, spinning on his heel to peer around the cabin. And he follows the same trail of thought I did—that if she's out in the mountains without gear, she must have back up.

"Angelo," he snarls, and I watch her face carefully.

Nothing. No flinch of fear. At least—no more than we've already put in her. Roxy Williams lies still, her eyes gone distant. Her forehead is beaded with sweat.

She's in pain.

Good. Fine. Not *good* that she's in pain, but *good*—I have a clear next step. I take the first aid kit and cross to the bed, lowering to sit on the mattress near her feet.

"Do you have any head injuries?" I murmur to her as Dante paces around the cabin, ranting under his breath about his brother. Roxy shrugs, not even looking at me.

Shit. We really are assholes.

"We won't hurt you." She looks at me then, scathing disbelief in her navy blue eyes as I shift forward, probing softly through her hair. "We're... this is perhaps an overreaction." Her eyes widen, like she can't believe what I'm saying, but I push on. Her hair is so soft, and there are lumps on her skull from the fall she

19

took. "These mountains aren't safe. And you chose the worst possible cabin to break in. Dante is very... cautious. He has good reason to be."

Roxy's eyes have drifted back to the center of my chest, the focus leaving them again. And that's not good—I want her present, fighting back, not drifting away into this bleak acceptance.

"Here." I tug the gag over her head before I can overthink it. "We need you to speak, anyway."

She licks her lips. "That is so generous of you." Her voice is cracked and hoarse already. My gut twists. "Thank you, Mister Kidnapper."

'Mister Kidnapper' is better than 'Alec', so I don't correct her. I move down her body, checking for cuts and broken bones.

"Did Angelo send you?" I ask casually. The injuries may be real, but her story is still bullshit. *No one* goes for a pleasure hike on the Lonely Mountain. Especially not without any gear.

"Who?" I watch her closely, but she's barely listening. Too busy hissing and wincing as I prod at her ribs.

"Angelo."

Again, nothing. Either she's an incredible actress or he really didn't send her. Because anyone who knows Angelo Marino does *not* forget his name.

He's a psychopath. A rabid dog with a bone.

Across the room, Dante groans, dragging a hand through his hair.

"No, I don't know some fucker called Angelo. Will you let me go now? Look, if you just untie me and let me leave, I won't press charges, I swear. I won't even mention you guys. Deal?"

It's tempting. So tempting. Especially when she looks at me with such hope, leaning forward an inch like she doesn't even realize it.

We could undo this right now. Set her loose again—god knows she probably won't last the night alone in the mountains with the state she's in—and plead ignorance if she ever tries to accuse us. We'd have time to sweep the cabin, to remove any evidence, and she's just had a fall. Any good lawyer would point out—she could have hallucinated all of this.

It's not a bad option.

If the slightest attention might not draw the Marinos here. And I don't believe for a second that she wouldn't report us—she's just saying what we want to hear.

We can't let Roxy go. But a ridiculous part of me still wants her to *understand.* I tear open an antiseptic wipe, cleaning a cut on her hip with tender hands.

"We won't hurt you," I repeat, though it sounds hollow, even to my ears. Aren't we already hurting her, scaring her like this? Keeping her against her will? "We just need to be sure."

"Sure of *what?*" she asks, her voice raised and thin, and Dante strides over, snatching up the gag. Roxy strains away, her teeth clenched shut, panic sparking in her eyes, and I speak quickly.

"Leave her."

Dante stares at me, stretched across her body. She's dwarfed by his shoulders, by the bulk of his chest. "Excuse me?"

Maybe his polite psycho act worked with his family, but I'm already too tired for his bullshit. "Leave her," I snap again. "No more gags."

"You were the one—"

"*Dante.*"

He clams up, a muscle ticking in his stubbled jaw.

I talk quietly. Calmly. Enunciating each word for them both to hear.

21

"We're going to treat her injuries. Check out her story. Then if she's telling the truth... we'll go from there. Alright?"

"No," Roxy says, as Dante hisses in response.

Good. Great. Glad we're all in agreement.

What a fucking day.

* * *

The moon hangs swollen above the trees when I finally step out onto the deck. I just need a moment—need to catch my breath away from Dante's loud brooding and Roxy's sarcastic remarks.

She's vicious when she wants to be. And I know we can't blame her, but part of me regrets the no-gag rule already.

The breeze is scented with pine and crisp snowfall from further up the mountain. I breathe deeply, feeling the throbbing in my head begin to subside, and listen to the wind shiver through the trees.

An owl hoots. Something scurries over the pine needles.

We're okay. Somehow... we'll make this okay.

"You're tired." The deck creaks as Dante joins me, resting one hand on the wooden rail. He stares up at the stars, his face as smooth and relaxed as if we'd spent the day fishing.

The Marinos.

That goddamn family.

"Why don't you head back?" Dante asks, and he says it like an offer. Like he'll take care of this. But I know what he's really asking: whether I trust him not to hurt her.

"And do what?" Bitter amusement curls my mouth. "Take a nap? Make dinner? I'm in this now, Dante." I turn to him, gripping the railing. "I'm not walking away. I'm part of this."

And I hope he can hear what I'm saying—that I trust him, yes, but I couldn't look myself in the eye ever again if I just left Roxy in there. Not with him, not with *anyone*.

Dante swallows and turns back to the stars, eyes bleak.

"If it's Angelo…" he says quietly. He doesn't finish that thought. He doesn't need to.

If Dante's brother has tracked him here, only one of them will leave alive. And though Dante hates and fears Angelo as much as any sane man, I'm not sure he could do it. If he could kill his own blood.

There was never much Marino in Dante. He never quite had their savage glee.

"I don't want her hurt," he says suddenly. "Even if she's helping Angelo. She probably doesn't have a choice."

I stand on the deck, watching the man I chased around the world and then somehow settled on the mountain with. And a tight knot I hadn't noticed eases in my chest.

"Good. I don't want that either."

"So we'll figure it out. And if he's found me… we'll run."

He hates that it comes out like a question. Dante jerks his head to the side, like he can shake off this sudden vulnerability.

"Yeah." I grip his shoulder and squeeze, my knuckles so close to the warmth of his throat. "We'll run. Start over again on a different mountain."

We. Together. I won't stay behind.

That's what he's asking, though he should know it by now. Where Dante goes, I go, and vice versa. I'm not sure how we got here, but what's done is done.

Dante grunts. "Somewhere warmer next time." But he's stepping closer, a hand raising to cup my elbow. The moment

23

pulls taut between us—months and years of tension twisting tight.

"I'll check on Roxy." I slip away, his warmth washing over my chest, and then the moment's gone.

Coward.

My boots drum over the deck.

Because I can't deal with that right now. The... *thing* between Dante and I. Everything that's unsaid.

One life-changing mess at a time.

4

Roxy

"So." I wince as the calm guy wraps my ankle in a bandage, the pads of his fingers so careful on my leg. "You kidnap often?"

He ignores me, focused on his work, his nimble fingers tying a perfect knot. He's so steady. So focused. I haven't really been banged up like this before, but I imagine if I had, this is the guy I'd have wanted looking after me.

You know. Apart from the whole tying-me-to-the-bed-frame thing.

He's just so *tender.* So gentle that it makes my chest ache, and makes bitterness clog my throat. Because he has no freaking right to be this way with me. No right to act like he *cares.*

I don't want to bond with these assholes. I want to get out this nightmare, limp to freedom, and write the travel article that will make my career.

Kidnapped on Lonely Mountain.

It has a certain ring to it.

Yeah. If I get out of this, they've done me a huge favor. And the longer they keep me here, the clearer it is that they don't want to hurt me. Despite the guns I've glimpsed on both of them, they don't seem to have the stomach for violence.

Well. That Dante guy... he might have shot me, at first. But his friend here keeps him on a tight leash.

"It's Alex, right?"

"Alec," he corrects quietly, checking the bandages lay flat. I take the opportunity to examine him closely—really commit him to memory for the police sketch.

He's tanned. Rugged. Mid thirties; a mix of golden skin and tawny hair and green eyes. It's a warm blend which makes him seem old fashioned, somehow. Like one of those old tourism posters.

"Probably should have given me a fake name."

Alec sighs heavily, flicking a glare at the other man. The loud one with the accent. "Probably."

Stretched out on the bed like this with him looming over me, it's impossible not to think certain thoughts. And in other circumstances, Alec is exactly the kind of guy I'd like leaning close and pinning me down. His touch is precise and efficient; he handles my body with a confidence that makes my skin flush. And his voice is deep and rich, with that delicious manly timbre. Not scratched up and strangled like mine right now.

Plus he smells really freaking good. Like woodsmoke and fresh rain.

Focus, you idiot.

"So what's the plan, Alec?" I prod him with my uninjured foot. "You gonna keep me here like a stray puppy? Gonna kill me? Or you gonna keep me trussed up like some weird sex slave?" My traitorous cheeks heat as I add that last bit, and a snort sounds across the room.

Dante leans against the wall, his arms crossed over his chest, his dark eyes glittering as he watches me. "Don't get your hopes up, Roxy Williams."

I flip him off, my hands still tied to the bed frame. "Eat me."

Dante smirks, his face sharp with vicious delight. "You wish."

"Children," Alec mutters, sounding one thousand years old. And where does this guy get off, acting like I'm the problem?

"I know," I say brightly, kicking him off the bed. Alec stands, palms raised, then crosses to the simple kitchen in the corner of the room. A faucet splutters as he fills a glass with water. "How about you two fuckers go jump off the mountain. And I'll wait here for the bear to get me."

"Oh, yes." Dante cocks his head. "This bear. The one who pushed you off a cliff and stole your backpack."

"I never said—"

"He sounds like a very mean bear."

"I'd take him over you two psychos any day."

"Perhaps you should have."

"Maybe I *will*."

"Enough." Alec's voice echoes through the cabin. He stands by the sink, pinching the bridge of his nose. "Please, you two, for the sake of my sanity, shut the hell up. Or I'll gag you *both*."

My neck twinges as I whip around to watch Dante's reaction. He doesn't seem like the kind of guy you threaten to gag. He seems like the kind of guy who'd slit your throat then brush a speck of lint off his sleeve. But Dante doesn't glower like I expect—he perks right up, straightening against the wall, clearly thrilled by the suggestion.

When he catches my eye, his face shutters. He leans back against the wall, sullen again.

"Oh. *Oh*." I grin at my captor, blowing a stray hair out of my face. "I get it now. Damn, that's awkward. Does he know,

Dante?"

"Shut the fuck up."

"Do I know what?" Alec asks, still rubbing his temples.

"Nothing," I say sweetly. "Nothing at all."

In normal circumstances, I would never be cruel about something like this. But in normal circumstances, I'm not lashed to a bed frame with two hot psychos pacing around arguing about what to do with me.

All's fair in war. And besides, I need all the leverage I can get.

"I won't say anything," I offer, holding Dante's eye. His hand twitches towards his gun. "Not if you let me go now."

"There's nothing to say."

"Sure there's not."

"Gags," Alec grits out. "Both of you."

I settle back against the thin pillows, mouth curled in a smirk. Alec won't let him hurt me, and now Dante has something to fear.

Good. Okay. I can work with this.

Freedom, here I come.

* * *

Two hours later, I break the silence again.

"I need to pee."

No, I don't. Not really. My body has been in fight-or-flight mode since the second I saw that bear. As far as I can tell from the clenched knot of my abdomen, I may never pee again.

But I've been planning. Scheming. And I need to get one of them alone.

Alec's already pushing to his feet, rolling his stiff neck, ready to escort me outside like the kidnapper gentleman he is. But it's Dante that strides to the bed, tugging the ties on my wrists undone with a flourish.

Oh, goody.

"Allow me." His cold smile makes my stomach flip. I swallow, throat suddenly dry, and swing my feet off the bed.

"Um, okay. Ow. Oh, shit. Ow ow ow." Blood rushes into my injured ankle, shocking the nerve endings into riotous life. I hop on one boot, tears swimming in my eyes, and I have no choice but to grab Dante's shoulder. His collarbone is sturdy under my hand, his firm muscles like rock. I guess chopping firewood makes you buff.

"Don't be a baby," he snaps, but he winds one arm around my waist. Supports me as I hop towards the door. I don't ask him to put my boot back on. It'd be like trying to squash a grapefruit into an egg cup.

He smells like woodsmoke, same as Alec, but different too. Like the ghost of expensive cologne.

The cabin is sparse. It's a small mercy: there's not much distance between the bed and the door. It's open plan, all one big room, with a kitchenette tucked in one corner and a sofa and coffee table placed together. Bookshelves line one wall, crammed with sagging paperbacks, and coarse gray curtains have been tugged shut. The only bursts of color are the patchwork bedspread and the faded burgundy sofa.

It doesn't suit Dante.

This is a man who seems like he'd be more at home in a penthouse. With stainless steel surfaces and marble counter tops.

"Watch my rug," Dante snaps as I scuff up the corner. It's paled with dust, but there's a paisley pattern woven into the fabric.

"Sorry," I mutter under my breath so only Dante can hear. "It's *such* a nice rug." My hand moves as I talk, sliding around his back—

Dante turns, angling his gun out of reach.

"Bad captive." He flicks my nose, and it's so unexpected that I blink. Behind me, Alec laughs softly on the sofa, and okay. Maybe he's just as bad as this asshole.

But then Dante leans in, his breath tickling my ear, and murmurs: "You go for my gun again, and I shoot your other foot. Understand?"

My teeth chatter as I nod, a wave of fear washing me under. Chilling me to my bones.

They're dangerous. I can't forget that. Only a few hours ago, Dante planned to shoot me. He *meant* it.

"Not so cute when Alec can't hear, are you?" We squeeze through the doorway, shuffling sideways like a messed up tripod.

"No." Dante's hand tightens on my waist. "And Alec has to leave sometimes."

My stomach twists, sweat breaking out down my spine. One minute at a time. I just need to get through this one minute at a time, but my plan was to speak to Alec alone. Not this asshole.

"Here." We pause at the steps, and Dante scoops an arm under my legs. He lifts me against his chest like I weigh nothing—just another piece of firewood—and I'm reminded again how fragile I am around these two.

Physically, anyway. Mentally, I'm pretty sure I can take them on. Especially when they're so clearly tangled up over each other, throwing those wistful glances when the other isn't looking—

"So how long have you been in love with Alec?"

30

Dante drops me without warning. I barely manage to land on my good leg, and the only thing that keeps me from toppling to the dirt is my hand clutching his sleeve.

"You can pee here."

"I asked you a question."

"And I ignored it."

I squint around the darkness, trying to make sense of the shadows. The moonlight washes the mountain in silver light, the blanket of stars adding an extra glow. And as my eyes adjust, I see the harsh set of Dante's face.

Time to stop prodding that wound.

"You don't have an outhouse or something? You just shit in the woods? That's gross."

"I have an outhouse," he clips out. Yeah, this guy is used to ensuite bathrooms. The fact that he has an *outhouse* clearly pains him. "But you're not using it. You're staying out in the open, where I can keep an eye on you."

"Pervert," I mutter, peeling down my shorts. "I knew you were weird." Dante's mouth twitches as he steadies my elbow, peering out into the dark trees. He keeps one hand on his gun, like he's expecting wildlife.

Bears… or something else.

Peeing is undignified. Clumsy. And it turns out I *can* go after all, for an awkwardly long amount of time.

"Goodness," Dante mutters dryly after two minutes. "Such an impressive show."

I glance at him quickly, but he's not watching, thank god. And I take my time fixing myself up and getting dressed again, pulling my shorts slowly up my legs.

"You know," I murmur once I'm covered again, "we could make some sort of deal."

31

"Oh?" He winds his arm back around my waist. Helps me to hop away to a clean patch of dirt.

"Yeah. Listen. I could help you out. Could help you make Alec jealous, or—or help you tell him how you feel. And in return, I limp off into the sunset and never speak of this to anyone. What do you think?"

"You won't tell anyone?"

I exhale sharply. Is this crap actually working? "No. Of course not." I mean, kidnappers are always a bit deluded, right?

"You don't like to post things online? People live on the internet these days."

"No!" I hop closer, a bubble of hope growing inside me. "No, never. I'm not even on social media," I lie. "I won't tell a soul."

"How wonderful," Dante says warmly. Then pauses. "But what about your travel blog?"

The grin freezes on my face. Warps into a grimace.

"What—how did you—"

"You've been with us for hours, Roxy," he says softly. "Did you not think we'd look you up?"

My lies from the last few minutes ring in my ears. My claims that I'm not on social media—oh god, I have so many accounts—my stupid *deal*.

"No." Dante squeezes my waist. From anyone else, it might be comforting. "Sorry, bella. No deal. And," he pauses, dragging me to a stop beside him. I turn to stone as something hard and cold prods my rib cage. "Fuck with me again and I will lose my patience, Alec or no Alec. Do you understand?"

I force myself to nod. A bird screeches nearby. The cold breeze slaps against my flushed cheeks.

"Good!" He's suddenly brisk again. Almost cheerful. "Well, that's done." He hitches me against his side and I flinch.

It was a dumb idea. And now I've shown my hand. Been caught in a lie when I'm trying to win their trust.

I stare at the ground all the way back to the cabin.

This is so messed up.

5

Dante

When I came out here to the mountains, when I left my life and family name behind, I did not intend to break any more laws.

Okay, maybe a couple. Small, stupid ones, like parking laws. And then there are the artworks I trade anonymously online—my one indulgence on this bleak mountainside, my one sip of culture in this world of corduroy and plaid. But nothing that could draw any attention to me. Nothing that would tatter the last scraps of my soul.

With Roxy…

This is not what I intended.

I lean my elbows on the railing that surrounds my cabin deck, squinting out into the darkness. It's late, the night silent except for the whispering breeze, and somewhere miles away, a wolf's ghostly howl bounces around the mountainside.

I'm exposed out here. If Angelo is near, he will see me. He'd have a clear shot too, but that's not his style.

Too quick. Too merciful. No chance to catch up and relive old times. No chance to make me *suffer*.

"Should you be out here?" Alec leans in the doorway behind me, his arms crossed over a faded red sweater. It's cold here at night, the temperature plummeting. Plenty of hapless hikers get caught off guard, coming here with no clue what it takes to survive.

Just like the hiker currently tied to my bed.

"She really is just a tourist," I mutter. I'm sure of it.

Roxy doesn't have the manner of someone who knows Angelo Marino. She's not haunted or twitching at every shadow. She's pissed off, sure, scared by her situation, but she doesn't know bone-deep terror. Not really.

Alec sighs. "Yes." He's been running background checks all night, using the satellite connections and calling up old contacts, and there are only a few checks left to do. But we both know already what they'll say.

She's innocent. A travel blogger with the worst kind of luck.

An injured young woman who we held hostage and threatened with a gun. Wonderful.

"Just because she doesn't know Angelo doesn't mean she can't cause you trouble." The way Alec says it is so casual. He's testing me. He wants to know what I'm going to do with her—whether I'll sacrifice Roxy to stay hidden from my family. And *when* will he stop testing me, exactly?

"We'll be long gone by the time press gets hold of it."

I swear, the temperature behind me warms two degrees. "Right." Two boot steps creak on the deck, then a hand grips my shoulder. And it takes everything inside me not to lean into Alec's touch. Not to turn and grip his wrist, to make him *acknowledge* this thing between us.

"You're a good man, Dante."

I snort. "Tell that to my captive."

"I wouldn't want to wake her."

"She's asleep?" I turn, surprised. She can't be *that* scared of us then, surely? The thought makes my chest pinch, and I rub at my sternum absentmindedly.

Rough flannel scrapes under my palm.

Seriously—fuck these mountain clothes.

"One day I will wear fine cotton again," I declare, dropping my hand and wiping my palm on my jeans. "And I will wash in a power shower, not in a river, and I will sip espresso in a courtyard by the sea."

The shadowed outline of Alec tilts his head.

"Is it really so bad here?"

No.

Not with you.

Except... we've been out here for almost two years. Cut off from the world, just the two of us. And while it took time to trust each other, to warm up and settle into some kind of friendship, that's all it's ever been.

Dancing around each other. Coming so close, then darting away.

We've stalled. Hit a rock face.

Maybe it's time to move on.

"Dante."

I blink, coming out from the tangle of my thoughts. "No. No, the mountains are fine, even if I need to dress like a rag doll."

Back home, I wore tailored suits. Fine colognes and heavy watches. My father bought me sapphire cuff links for my eighteenth birthday without a hint of irony.

I still have them, hidden inside the cabin. Insurance, for the next escape.

"We'll take her into town." Alec is in list-mode. It calms him.

"Leave her with mountain rescue. Then head straight out of state, swapping vehicles, changing names—you know the drill."

"I do."

"We can't leave any hints behind. We'll need to sweep your cabin. There'll be no sleep tonight."

"Nope. Only for Roxy."

He quietens at her name. He's soft on her too—I've seen the way his eyes snag on her every time he glances in her direction. The way his mouth twitches at her outrageous insults; the tender way he checks her wounds.

Maybe he should stay behind. Stay with *her*.

I shake myself. Roxy wouldn't want *either* of us. This endless day is getting to me.

"This is the worst thing I've done," he tells me quietly. And that's something, right? From an ex FBI agent who moved in a mile from his mark.

"I've done it. Not you."

"No." Alec's eyes burn in the moonlight. "Don't do that. Don't give me an out. I did this too, and one day I'll pay for it."

"One day," I repeat softly. Not today.

And if I have any say in it, that day will never come. I would do anything for this man. Anything.

I've never had true family before.

When we step back inside, I can't resist wandering to the bedside. Roxy's arms are tied above her head, her cheek pillowed against her bicep, and is that uncomfortable?

Too late now.

Her dark hair spills over the pillow and her shoulders, loose strands lying across her cheek. Her forehead is smooth in sleep, as though she's not held captive at all. As though she's tucked up safely at home, cozy and sweet. I press my mouth together as I unlace her other boot, tugging it gently off her foot. She stirs, mumbling something, then drifts straight back to sleep.

I place the boot beneath the bed. Swipe the blanket from the back of the sofa.

It's cold in the mountains. Even with a fire crackling in the wood burner by the sofa, the chill creeps through the room. Alec is bundled in layers over by the wooden desk, urging our ancient computer to make it through the night. And Roxy's cheek is cool when I brush it with the back of my knuckles, smoothing her hair away.

I spread the blanket over her. Pretend I don't feel Alec's eyes on me as I tuck her in, make sure she's covered. Then, when I've run out of excuses to linger, I drag myself away and start packing up the cabin.

Just the essentials. Any identifying items.

And I do it all quietly, so I don't wake our guest.

6

Angelo

My brother always had the same weakness: impulse control. He's hot-headed, a Marino through and through, even when he runs off to play hideaway in the mountains. Dante could make the perfect plan, make it watertight, then ruin it at the last second with a tiny impulse.

For example: Dante would disappear. Have a charred body falsely matched with his dental records. Let our family *mourn*, weeping over the closed casket at his funeral.

Then he'd start a new life. Some ridiculous peasant existence in the mountains, and he'd hate his new trappings, and his impulses would win out.

Like impulses to trade art online. To keep a fingertip in the world he supposedly left.

I sigh, shaking my head, and hop down off my rocky ledge. A backpack slumps upside down in the dirt, but I'm not interested in some wayward hiker. After almost two years, I've found my big brother.

Nothing else matters.

He's not alone. That was the first thing I noticed today, when

I picked my way through the trees in the dying light. I traced him all the way from the east coast to this godforsaken cabin, and when I get there, he has *company*.

The least Dante could do is be lonely. Soul-shakingly lonely, like I've been.

It's fine. He'll pay for every insult, every day he let me think he was dead.

There is at least one person, possibly two. The curtains are drawn, and I can't be sure.

They will pay too.

For stealing my brother. For taking *my* family, and keeping him here, away from me. For being his *first fucking choice*, it's insult after insult, and I'm breathing hard through my nose. So loud I'll freak out the wildlife.

So—okay. I suck in a long, slow breath and hold it for the count of five. And when I gust it out again, my head is clear, my heartbeat slowing to a dull tick. I pick my way back down the path, back towards the cabin that is already fixed in my mind.

I won't go charging in, gun drawn. It's not my style. And I'd hate to disappoint Dante after all this time. No—there are ways we do things. The Marinos are creatures of tradition, and I honor mine, pulling the small black business card from my jacket pocket. It looks out of place against my outdoorsman's outfit—all rough, sturdy materials and warm layers.

God, how does Dante stand it? The chafing alone must drive him insane.

"Hello, big brother," I murmur, my steps silent on the deck. I go right to the door and place it on the floorboards—I want him to know how close I've been. Then I pause, straining for voices, but all I hear is the crackle of a fire and the tap of keys.

More art trading, perhaps. Oh, Dante.

He can tell me all about it soon.

7

Roxy

The first thing Alec does when I wake up is untie my hands. Jeez, I can't believe I slept at all. I'm lucky they didn't harvest my organs or something. I blink up at him, eyes bleary, as he leans over me, surrounding me with his woodsman scent.

"Wha—Alec?"

He tugs the ties free, mouth set in a hard line. His green eyes are shadowed, his tan face ashen, but my stomach doesn't twist. Apparently my body missed the memo about being afraid.

"Good morning, sunshine." Dante smirks as he strides past, stuffing something in a duffel bag. I gape around the cabin as I sit up, only just noticing the wreckage.

It looks like a tornado blew through here.

The desk drawers hang open. Books slump sideways on the shelves. The kitchen cupboard doors hang wide, displaying their half-empty shelves of canned goods and instant coffee. Blue-tinged dawn light glows around the edge of the curtains, and the fire in the wood burner has died down to embers.

"Um. Hi." What else do you say to your cheery captor? I rub

at my sore wrists, rolling my neck. "Am I peeing?"

"You tell us." Dante winks at me, and Alec stifles a laugh. And what the hell is this, exactly? Happy families?

"Hilarious," I snap. "So, tell me, kidnappers. What's the plan for today? Going to abduct more innocent women? Try your hand at murder?"

"No." The brief amusement has drained from Alec's face. He picks up my ankle, probing gently at the bandages, and apparently I'm still bleary from sleep because I *let* him. I even shuffle closer so he can check it properly. "We're driving into town. Dropping you off with mountain rescue."

I peer at him, waiting for the punch line. It doesn't come.

"You guys are weird."

"Would you rather we killed you?" Dante asks, but not like it's a threat. Like it's funny I'm arguing.

"No. Obviously not."

"Then you're welcome."

"You—"

"Please." Alec holds up a palm, and we both fall quiet. "Not today."

Silence reigns for all of two minutes. Then I mumble, "I don't understand."

Alec leans down and scoops up my boot, balancing my leg on his knee. I studiously ignore the hard muscle of his thigh, the way his worn jeans cling to the lines of his legs, as he loosens my bootlaces as wide as they'll go.

"We made a mistake," he mutters. "We misread the situation, Roxy. We're sorry."

My laugh bites off as he slides my foot into my boot. The swelling has gone down a bit since last night, but it still hurts like a bitch.

43

"You're sorry? Oh! Oh, that's okay then."

"Save it for your blog," Dante snaps. "Let's go."

"No breakfast in bed? No guest book to sign?" Now I'm just being a brat, although the stew Alec cooked last night *was* delicious. My stomach growls loudly at the memory, and I huff as I shove my other boot on and stand up, hopping on one leg and leaving the last of my dignity on the bed. Alec wraps an arm around my waist, holding me at more of a distance than Dante did.

"Two hours," is all he says. "It's a two hour drive. Then we'll drop you in town and you can get all the food you want."

"And you guys?"

His face smooths blank. "We'll come back here."

I snort. "Yeah, right. You're a terrible liar. You two aren't coming back."

"Will you miss us?" Dante asks slyly, shouldering his duffel and wrenching the door open.

He freezes. There's no other word to describe it. One second, his cheeks are bunched from grinning, his shoulders more relaxed than I've ever seen him. Then he frosts over, every line of him going taut, the smile wiped off his face.

"What is it?" Alec steps away from me immediately, striding to the doorway and peering over Dante's shoulder. He goes still.

"For fuck's sake," I say loudly. "What is it? You assholes." I start to hop closer, determined to see, my arms spread wide and wobbling.

"Stay back," Alec barks, and I falter. "Roxy. Stay away from the windows and the door. Keep out of sight."

"But—"

"Do it!"

44

I flop onto the sofa, more shocked by Alec's sudden commanding tone than anything else. For the first time in hours, sweat breaks out on the backs of my knees. My heart thumps faster.

Danger.

Something is very wrong.

Dante bends stiffly, picking something up from the deck. He pinches it between his thumb and forefinger, holding it at arm's length like it might detonate.

"A business card?" I ask.

No one answers.

"But she's clean," Alec mutters. "I checked everything. There's no way she knows him—"

"Coincidence, then." Dante glances at me, and for the first time there is true regret in his eyes. "Or very bad luck."

"Do you think he's seen her?"

"Who?" I call, even as a name flashes across my mind. *Angelo.*

The mysterious Angelo. The man who scares these men so much that they took me captive. Just *in case.*

"It doesn't matter. Either he sees us drive her into town, or he sees us leave her here." Dante scowls at the business card. "She's safer with us."

They're still stood in the doorway. Right there in the open. If they're so scared, why don't they get out of sight too? I open my mouth to say so, but Alec grabs his own bag, all business.

"We go now. I'll cover you until you get Roxy in the truck. Then—"

"He'll have cut the brakes."

They fall silent, chests heaving.

"My truck," Alec clips out. "He'll have seen me. But he might not know where I live."

45

"It's half a mile away. He'll be watching already, it's too risky—"

"So distract him." Alec glances at me, and something about the way he stares makes my stomach clench. Like he's saying goodbye. He looks at Dante the same way, then drops his bag back to the floor.

"Bring it if you can," he mutters, then strides back through the cabin to the back door. He takes the handle and pauses, waiting for something.

"Roxy." Dante crosses the rug. He pulls me up from the sofa where I'm sprawled, too confused and scared to follow what's happening. "It's going to be okay, bella." His accent gets thicker when he's worried. Does he know that? "We're going to create a little distraction."

"What about staying out of sight?" I hop across the floorboards, clinging tight to Dante's shoulder. His shirt is thick and soft, a chequered red flannel, and I have the bizarre urge to bury my face in it until this is all over.

"Not going to work. He'll see you either way."

"Angelo?"

Dante's jaw works. "Yes. Angelo. Here." He pauses in the doorway and scoops me up bridal style, the floor dropping out from beneath me.

I catch one final glimpse of Alec over Dante's shoulder, then I'm carried out into the bright dawn light.

* * *

"Who is Angelo?" I whisper as Dante strolls across the deck. His posture is relaxed and languid again—a big ol' *fuck you* to whoever is watching. But I can feel his heart thumping in his

46

rib cage; can feel the tremor in his rock-hard muscles.

"Don't say his name," he murmurs, pretending to smell my hair. "Don't even whisper it."

"But he left his card. He knows we found it—"

"Enough questions, Roxy." Dante sets me on the railing, stepping between my thighs. "We have a job to do."

Right. A distraction. While Alec… what? Gets his truck? How far away is it? Will we know if he gets caught? What if this *Angelo* knows about that truck too—

"Smile," Dante murmurs. He traces his thumb over my cheek. "Or at least don't scowl at me like that. We're trying to put on a show."

"What kind of show?" I ask, even as Dante nudges closer between my legs. His hips slot against mine, the warmth of his body washing over my core, and I swallow hard. "Oh."

"My brother was never good at relationships," Dante murmurs, dragging the tip of his nose up my hairline. I wrap my arms around his neck, tipping my face up to the pale blue sky, and my eyelids flutter closed of their own accord. "Too unnerving. He set everyone on edge."

"So we're making him jealous?"

"Something like that."

My breath hitches. "We're making him *angry*?"

Dante hums. "We want his full attention."

My hands roam down Dante's back. I find his gun again, my fingertips drifting over the hard ridge of it, but this time he doesn't angle away.

"You take it if you need it." He speaks the words against my throat. "Do you know how to use it?"

My fingers curl away. "No."

Dante sighs, and it's not fake arousal. It's the sound of

47

exhausted regret. "Roxy. What have we done to you?"

I don't know how to answer that. Don't know how to process *any* of this. Mere hours ago, this man held me at gun point. He tied me to a bed and wouldn't let me leave. Now we're together somehow, cooperating against some mysterious enemy, and the press of his lips against my throat sends sparks racing over my skin.

This is fucked up. So messy, so surreal, and is it even really happening? Is this just another mind game? My back arches, pushing me closer, pressing my breasts against the hard planes of his chest.

"Very good," Dante says, voice ragged. "Very convincing." A hand slides into my hair, scratching gently at my scalp. "He'll think I tempted a sweet hiker to my cabin."

"Instead of locking her inside."

Dante shrugs, the movement rocking me on the railing. "You did break a window."

A giddy burst of laughter travels up my throat. It's not really funny—none of this is funny—but I've been wound so tight for so long now that I'm bursting at the seams. I'm held together by a thread, ready to howl with laughter or scream or burst into tears at any moment.

"Dante," I manage, voice strangled. He pulls back and looks at me, and my breath catches at what I see.

His pupils are blown wide, his eyes nearly black. His olive cheeks are flushed darker, his pulse thrumming in his throat.

He wants me. Or his body does, anyway. It's responding to this, the same as mine.

It's the danger. The adrenaline.

That's all.

"My article is going to be insane."

48

He jerks back slightly then smiles, his eyes crinkling. And the warmth that spreads over his handsome face—it's like the rising sun cresting over the mountaintop.

"Yes, bella. No more lies between us. You will write your article and it will be insane."

I raise an eyebrow. "I'll be famous."

He nods. "If you want to be."

Doesn't everyone want to be famous? I kind of figured that was a given, but now I'm not so sure. Not with the tired resignation in Dante's eyes.

"Are you famous?" It's all starting to make sense. Or not—not *sense*, never that, but I'm piecing things together. Why he thought I broke in on purpose. Targeted him out of everyone.

"In a way. My family is well known."

"Who are your family?"

"The Marinos."

I freeze, my hands looped around Dante's neck. He looms in front of me, so broad, so tall, so *solid*. His dark eyes watch me closely; his breath fans over my cheeks.

"The..."

"Yes. You've heard of us?"

I nod, lips numb.

Holy shit. I broke a mobster's window.

"I..."

"Oh, Roxy." Dante sighs. Rubs my bare forearm below my rolled sleeve. "You've gone so wooden on me. It's rather late to develop a survival instinct now."

The morning breeze drifts over the deck. Tugs at my hair and slips down the neck of my sweater. I shiver, pulling Dante closer automatically, and though surprise flashes over his face, he crowds me against the railing.

49

"When will Alec come back?" I murmur against his throat. Again, I scent something beneath the woodsmoke and pine. The ghosts of expensive grooming. "How far to the truck?"

"A few minutes more."

"How will we know if this is working?"

"We won't. Not until it's done."

"I don't..." I trail off, not sure what I'm saying. *I don't want to do this* sounds lame. *I don't want to die* is just so predictable. And besides, there are lots of things I don't want to do beside dying. Being abducted is still high on that list, although my firsthand experience of it hasn't been so bad. All in all, the bear gave me a worse time than this mobster.

I don't say that, obviously. Kidnappers don't need validation.

But I'm hit suddenly with the icy knowledge that this danger is real. That I could die out here on Lonely Mountain. They lulled me into feeling safe with their gentle hands and their banter. But this is something else—this is *Angelo*.

I bury my face in Dante's chest.

His palm rubs circles on my back. It's rhythmic, soothing, and I sway closer. Wrap my arms tight around his waist.

The roar of an engine makes Dante jerk to life. He scoops me off the railing and runs with me, pounding down the steps before I even process what's happening. There's a shout, the pop of gun shots, and then a truck door is thrown open and I'm bundled inside.

"Go!"

The door slams shut and the truck lurches away, bouncing so hard over the ground that my teeth snap together. I'm tossed around in the backseat, my ankle searing with pain, but when I try to struggle upright Dante pushes me back down.

"Stay low." His voice is rough. I peer through my hair, and

find him clutching one arm. A dark stain spreads beneath his grip, soaking his shirt and sticking it to his skin. Dante shifts until he's sitting in the center, leaning forward to mutter to Alec. And we bounce down the mountainside, one window shattered and light pouring through a bullet hole in the truck roof.

8

Alec

T he truck lurches beneath me, the engine roaring as we
pound down the rock face. We're sliding and veering,
glancing off outcrops, and there's no way my truck is
making it through this morning.

"Hold tight," I grit out, stating the obvious.

Dante doesn't give me shit for it. That's how freaked he is. He
leans between the front seats, one hand gripping my headrest,
his knuckles brushing against the back of my head.

"Is he following?" A voice pipes up from the backseat. A
glance in the rear view mirror shows Dante pushing firmly on
Roxy's shoulder, holding her down without looking. Good.

"He will."

If we're lucky, Angelo will have a short hike to his transport.
We might get a ten minute head start—maybe fifteen if we're
truly blessed.

Better make it count.

"Where are we going?"

"The nearest town."

"Won't he expect that?"

"Yes."

"Then why—"

I speak over her, my voice raised above the crashing truck and screaming tires. "Trust us, Roxy. You need to trust us. I know we don't deserve it, but I swear we'll keep you safe. And as soon as we're sure Angelo doesn't care about you, we'll let you go. Okay?"

She grumbles something, but it's drowned out by the thump of the truck down the dirt path. I lurch forward, bracing myself against the steering wheel.

It's shameful of me, but I fucking love driving like this. It was my favorite part of FBI training. Even now, with our lives on the line and Dante's feral brother snapping at our heels, vicious glee swarms in my chest. I wrench the wheel, slamming my boot flat on the gas.

Hell. Yes.

"Stop enjoying this," Dante murmurs, his voice soft yet cutting through the chaos. A knuckle rubs at my hair, and my heart pounds harder.

"You just worry about Roxy," I croak. In the mirror, I see him rubbing her shoulder. His thumb swipes back and forth over her bunched purple sweatshirt, soothing her, soothing us both, and the image of them wrapped around each other on the deck jabs at my brain.

My gut churns. It's ugly, this jealousy, and the worst part is I'm not even sure where it's directed. Who I'd want to take the place of in that tableau—whether I want Roxy crushed against my chest, her soft curves against my hardness, or Dante pressing me against the railing. And none of it fucking matters, since Roxy hates both our guts, and we could all die here anyway—

The truck rockets down a left fork in the path, bouncing

between the trees. In the distance, tents pitched by a creek flash bright red, blue and yellow between the trunks; the ground levels out beneath the tires.

"Trust me," I tell them again, then slam on the brakes. We screech to a stop, skidding over the dirt, smoke rising from under the hood. Then I turn in my seat, throw the truck in reverse, and veer off the path into a dark cave.

We barely fit. For one sickening moment, the truck wedges between the cave walls. Then I gun the engine and we shove inside, the truck doors buckling inward, pale blue paint left behind on the rock.

I kill the engine. It still whirs, cooling, smoke leaking into the gloom. We sit in the inky darkness, the only light spilling through the cave entrance twenty feet away, the only sound our ragged breaths.

"Sit up." Behind me, Dante pulls Roxy upright. He leans over and pops her door open a crack. "Be ready to run."

"My ankle—"

"It's a sprain, not a break. Run on it, Roxy."

I close my eyes as her breath hitches. "Okay."

We did this. We brought her here. If we'd believed her when we met her, if we just helped her like she wanted, she'd be miles away by now. Safely in town, with her foot properly bound.

She'll never forgive us. I hope she doesn't. Which stings worse than it should, because if we'd met Roxy any other way, if we'd gone for a drink in the town and seen her leaning at the bar...

I'd have talked to her. Tried to make her laugh.

It doesn't matter. Wishful thinking gets us nowhere.

Sounds echo in the cave. The *plink* of water, dripping further back in the darkness. The rustle of bat wings. The cooling *tick*

tick tick of the truck engine, overheated and overworked.

And our breaths. We're panting, all three of us, inhaling deeply through our noses as we try to calm down.

Out beyond the cave entrance, distant shouts echo from a picnic area. At the base of Lonely Mountain, the area gets a face lift. The air warms, the trees are greener, and the creek rolls lazily past, its earlier crushing rapids forgotten.

People bring their kids here. They play ball and cook hot dogs.

And now Angelo Marino is on the prowl.

"We can't stay here," Dante mutters, like he's just thought the same thing.

"A few more minutes."

"But—"

"Trust me."

We wait in the darkness, hyper aware of each other's bodies. Then: a distant roar. The thunder of heavy tires down the mountain path. If we made half the racket that Angelo's making, it's a wonder there are still kids nearby at all. If I were out there fishing or playing catch, you'd better believe I'd be running for cover.

"He's gone past," Roxy murmurs. "The sound's fading."

"Ten more minutes." I can *feel* them glancing at each other, sharing a doubtful look in the dark, but this is *my* background. I know men like Angelo. "He'll sense that he lost us. Then he'll backtrack up the mountain. Go down the other fork in the road."

"He'll come past the cave," Dante points out, always so reasonable. Never flustered—not by real danger. Only by terrible clothes.

"He won't notice."

"Angelo notices everything."

Maybe. Maybe I'm trapping us here, fish in a barrel, but it's too late to make another play. And when the engine roars back up the mountain, screeching even louder this time, Angelo's fury broadcast over the mountainside, we all freeze.

None of us breathe. None of us even twitch.

He crashes past, a symphony of tortured metal. The breath leaves my chest.

"Fuck," Dante mutters.

"Yeah," Roxy agrees. "Fuck."

"Let's go. Now." I kick my door open—no point in keeping quiet. Either Angelo is gone or we're dead anyway. "We go on foot. Blend with the crowds. There are tourist buses down off the mountain."

"I came in on one of those." Roxy shoves her door open with a grunt, wriggling to the edge of her seat. "It smelled like egg mayo." Dante's rounding the truck, going to lift her again, but I stride faster, beating him there.

"Your arm," I mutter. He doesn't buy it, and I avoid his eye as I hoist her against my chest.

He's hurt.

It's for the best.

* * *

Lonely Mountain isn't like the Grand Canyon or El Cap. It doesn't attract hordes of tourists with glossy brochures, or feature in Hollywood films. It's scenic, yes—so brutally beautiful it's hard to look at—but it's harsh, too. People die here, mobsters aside.

You don't just summit Lonely Mountain on a bucket list

whim.

If you want to climb it, you have to *earn* it.

But that's on the mountain proper, when you get up above the tree line, with your thighs burning as you push up into the thinning air. The real Lonely Mountain begins closer to the clouds than the ground.

At the base, though... it's summer camps and corporate retreats. Identical cabins and hourly boat rental on the pristine lake.

"I can't believe you're writing about this shit hole." Dante glowers at Roxy, still in a foul mood since I picked her up in the cave. She's back on the ground again, standing on her good foot as we line up for the bus, but it's my side she leans against.

Dante doesn't like that.

I do.

"I'm not writing about *this*." Roxy scowls back, affronted. "I was writing about the lower peaks. You know, the cool bit. Above the tourist trap and below all the death."

"You got pretty high."

"I'm not great at maps."

Dante scoffs. "How do you accidentally climb a mountain?"

"How do you mistakenly take someone captive?" she shoots back.

I hush them both, urging Roxy to shuffle down the line. We're exposed out here, and even though Dante's picking a fight, I know he feels it too. The lake shore is nearby, glittering sapphire in the sunshine, and it's sinister somehow. The laughs of children sound all wrong. Warped and shrill.

Adrenaline. It's normal, but it's instinct, too. Screaming at us that Angelo's still close, he could come back at any time, and if he sees us here, no one in this crowd will be safe.

"Back to town, folks?" The driver eyes us with blatant interest. And who can blame him? We look like a sight.

Roxy—bedraggled and hopping on one leg.

Dante, one palm clapped over his bloodstained sleeve.

And me, staring around us so hard that my eyes run dry. I blink, digging my wallet out of my back pocket.

"Please."

"You all together?" The guy's eyes are bugging out as he takes us in, standing too close to be normal. There's something lecherous about his tone, dripping with insinuation, and Dante's already bristling when Roxy pipes up.

"You got a problem with that?"

The driver jerks back: a bristled old man faced with a pint-sized firecracker of a woman. He wets his lip; shakes his head.

"No, ma'am."

He still looks scandalized, but Roxy just smirks as she loops her arm around my shoulder.

"Help me up, Alec," she murmurs, smooth as silk.

This is not the time. Not the time to mess with the bus driver; not the time to feel my blood rushing south. I grit my teeth and help her up, paying with the other hand, and I don't speak again until we're settled in the back row.

Me next to the window.

Roxy pressed against my thigh.

And Dante glowering in the center seat.

They start murmuring together, and I tune them out. I stare out at the lake, scanning the crowds for dark hair and amber eyes, and as the minutes pass and I don't see him, my pulse slows.

She's right. It does smell like egg mayo.

"What's the game plan?" A sharp elbow digs into my side.

58

Roxy's brown hair tickles my arm as she turns to me. "When we get to town. What's next?"

"We hide out. Let Angelo think we've left the area. Then get you to safety before we run."

She nods, chewing her lip, and I know it's wishful thinking, but she almost seems sad to leave us.

"Where will you go?"

"Why?" Dante interrupts. "Will you put it in your article? Tell the cops?"

"Maybe." She whirls around and glares. "You don't think you deserve it?"

He says nothing, the bus rumbling to life beneath us. Then, quietly: "Somewhere warm. By the sea."

It's impossible to miss the longing in his voice. He stares out at the glittering lake as the bus lurches around. And I'm glad when Roxy traces her fingertip over his wrist—a comfort neither of us deserve.

Dante clears his throat. Then very deliberately, he takes her hand, winding their fingers together.

My turn to stare out of the window. The trees blur past, and my eyes glare unseeing out of the smudgy tinted glass.

Lake shore and tree trunks.

It's a shitty goodbye.

9

Dante

A motel. A *motel.* Charged by the hour. My soul withers inside me as I push through our door. Roxy limps in next, supported by Alec, and I try not to dwell on the way she keeps choosing him. Leaning against him naturally, like it's as easy as breathing.

I should let him go too. Send him with her before I run.

There's still time for me to do it. To be a better man.

For now, though, there is this: the ultimate karmic punishment. Polystyrene bedspreads and a balding green carpet, dotted with cigarette burns. I wrinkle my nose at the dusty television set and stiff, heavy curtains, crossing to yank them closed with my uninjured arm.

The room dims. Closes in and turns impossibly gloomier.

"Well," Roxy chirps. "This is… nice."

"You didn't stay here before?" I murmur as Alec flicks on the light. It's weak, barely casting a glow over the carpet. No surprise. "Before your egg mayo bus ride?"

She raises her chin and doesn't deign to answer. Instead, she limps further into the room, nodding at the one single bed pushed against the faded wall.

"Dibs."

Alec and I both turn to the double. It juts out from the wall, taking up most of the floor.

"I don't..." he begins, but I talk over him.

"Perfect. Alec and I can spoon."

His cheekbones flush. It's nothing. Nothing. But Roxy slides me a sly smile, flopping onto her bed in a chorus of bedsprings, and I suddenly wish I'd kept quiet. I'm not used to this—having someone else around us. Someone who can read me; who notices the way my eyes linger on the other man.

I've fallen out of practice. If I'd let this slip around my family...

It's unthinkable. My skin goes clammy at the idea.

Alec gives me thirty minutes. Enough time to duck inside our bathroom, lock the door, and bite the hand towel as I peel my shirtsleeve off my wound. The pain sears my arm, makes my breath come faster, and when I catch sight of myself in the mirror, the tendons stand out harsh on my neck.

I drop the shirt on the tiles. Run the faucet with shaking hands, splashing cold water on my face, the back of my neck, my chest. Rivulets run over the dark hairs on my chest, on the tattoos inked into my olive skin.

Finally, dripping, I turn to the side. Hold my breath and splash water over my wound.

"Motherf—"

A knock rattles the bathroom door.

"Have you started without me? Dante, you asshole. Let me in."

It's fine. He can come in now—the worst is over. Hidden away. So I spin the lock, flashing a grin as Alec squeezes into the tiny bathroom with me.

61

"Did it stick?"

I nod at the pile of bloody, dried shirt. "Not for long."

He levels me a look. "Bet that hurt."

No point pretending otherwise. "Like a bitch."

I wait for the lecture. For him to say he could have helped; that it might have hurt less with two.

Alec wedges himself between me and the sink. He runs fresh water, his forehead creased in the mirror.

"The kit was in my bag. We're making do."

"It was the bags or Roxy," I say, even though he didn't ask.

"I know."

"I'm sorry."

"Don't be." Green eyes meet mine in the glass. "It's just stuff. It doesn't matter. Besides—" he turns without warning, and I jerk back but there's nowhere to go. Alec's chest brushes mine, shirt to bare skin, and can he feel my heart pounding through the fabric? "You're the one with the bullet wound."

"Just a graze." I twist and show him the outside of my bicep. The shot gouged out a track through my flesh, but that's all.

We got lucky. Or Angelo's going soft.

"I'll clean it." He peers closer, his face coming nearer to mine. "Water first, then the vodka from the mini bar. Roxy called the front desk asking for a needle and thread."

Shit. "And a lighter," I rasp.

This motel is so foul, I wish we could burn the whole building down first. Disinfect everything.

Alec nods. "And a lighter."

His touch is gentle but firm. Distant—like a doctor with a patient. It's worse, somehow, than him never touching me at all. A taunt. I stare up at the ceiling, at the blotchy pattern of water marks, as Alec methodically washes my wound.

"First Roxy's ankle, now you."

I hum. Nudge him with my boot. "Last man standing."

"Let's hope not." The pink-tinged water gurgles down the drain. We're done, no reason to linger, and yet neither of us moves. I watch the pulse thrumming in Alec's throat, too afraid to look away in case it slows.

"You don't need to be here, you know." *Here, with me.* I can't look at him when I say this. "You could stay with Roxy. She won't report you."

"I know." That's all he says. And it's so loaded, so unclear, that I could slam my head against the wall. In this stupid motel, it'd crumple like damp cardboard.

"This is where you say thank you," Alec says quietly.

My eyes slam shut. "Fuck you."

"Half right." Amusement curls through his voice, and strong fingers wrap around my wrist. My heart stops. "You were almost there, Dante. So close."

Cool air washes over my bare chest as Alec steps back into the bedroom, leaving me slumped against the counter.

So close?

He has no idea.

10

Angelo

I scratch the craggy cave entrance with my thumbnail, pale blue paint peeling off in slivers. Next to the light stone, it was easy to miss. If the truck had been red or black, I'd have found them right away.

It's no excuse.

"Dante," I breathe, clicking my tongue. "Big brother. Where are you hiding?"

They're not inside the cave. It's clear from the echoing silence, the chatter of sleepy bats in the velvet gloom. I go in anyway, dirt crunching under my boots, the air damp and musky in my nostrils.

Dante will have hated this. These bad smells. This wet, dirty mountain. He used to lose his mind over a fleck of dust on his sleeve; the last two years must have been torture.

A good place to hide, though. If I hadn't found his art trading activities, I'd never have looked here.

"Come out, come out," I sing-song, even though it's just me in the cave. A dress rehearsal, I suppose. I've been dreaming of this day, of finding my big brother again. Proving he's alive.

No one believed me. Well, now they will see.

A knot tightens in my chest, even though he's not here, even though this isn't real yet. And that tangle of nerves, it sets my teeth on edge.

He had no right. No right to hide from us; to make me hunt him like this.

Their truck is a shape in the dark. A thicker patch of shadows. I pluck my phone from my back pocket and turn on the flashlight. It beams over the battered hood; the scratched paint; the shredded tires. The bullet holes.

I didn't hit him. Not really. He was lined up perfectly, his broad chest in my view, and at the last second my hand twitched to the side. Out of my control. An impulse. A moment of weakness.

It won't happen again.

I flip the phone over in my palm, checking the time. Not yet noon. The day has barely begun. They won't have gone far, not yet, and even if they had—I'd find him. So I stroll back to the cave entrance, whistling quietly.

I could call home. Tell my father he was wrong—that Dante is alive. Like I've been saying, like I told them all a thousand times. But once it's confirmed, the whole family will mobilize. The whole network. The hunt won't be mine anymore.

No. I've earned this. Dante is *mine.* I'll be the one to bring him in, to bring him home.

He never should have left us.

Children's laughter echoes from the lakeside. I step out into the sunshine, blinking in the sudden brightness, and tug my jacket sleeves straight as I wander toward the crowds. An ice cream van pulls up, tinny theme song blaring.

I change direction, heading for the van.

There's no rush. I've got time.

11

Roxy

I hiss between my teeth, wincing as the needle digs into Dante's arm. Alec stitches slowly, his face stoic and his stitches neat, but he hates this. His shoulders are taut, the lines of his body rigid. The two of them sit on the edge of the double bed, Alec's expression wooden and Dante's smoothed blank.

He's doing the whole macho, I-don't-feel-pain thing. *Men.*

"Yowza." I lean closer, balancing on one leg. My ankle wobbles, and I grab Dante's shoulder.

"Do you mind?" he grinds out, and I don't know what he means—my hand or the way I'm watching, hissing and grimacing at every stitch. "I'm trying to ignore this. You're not helping."

"How about another distraction?" I blurt before I can think better of it.

It was strategic earlier. To keep Angelo's attention; I know that. It was pretty fun, though. In a verging-on-hysterics kind of way.

A muscle ticks in Alec's jaw. He draws the needle out

67

again, stern and silent, and Dante turns to me, eyes glittering. "Whatever do you mean?"

I must be half out my mind on adrenaline still, because I've got that rushing feeling. That giddy, top-of-the-rollercoaster sensation, where my stomach swoops but I don't want to stop, not for anything. It's the same feeling I get when I step off a plane in a new country. When I pack up my whole life and uproot myself on a whim.

They held me captive, yes. And I haven't forgiven them for that, but I'm also not scared of them anymore. They're pussycats.

"Like earlier." My hand fists Dante's shirt on his shoulder, straining it over the hard bulge of his muscle. He watches me, unblinking. "On the cabin deck." I swallow. "You liked it. I know you did."

His voice is velvet. "Remind me, Roxy."

I slide onto his lap with an *oof.*

The needle pauses on his other arm. Alec is rigid, turned to stone, but then he starts up again. *Prod, push, drag.* He stares at his line of stitches so intently, they should burst into flame.

Oh dear. Dante's not the only one with big feelings.

"This is not a good distraction." Dante raises an eyebrow, jerking me back to the present. I shuffle closer, winding my arms around his neck.

"You don't smell like the mountains."

His mouth quirks. "I'll take that as a compliment."

"Alec does."

His smirk fades. "Yes. He does."

"How disturbing," Alec murmurs. *Prod, push, drag.* "You've both been sniffing me."

"Big, greedy lungfuls," I assure him. Dante's eyes narrow. It's the only warning I get before he surges forward, trapping my bottom lip between his teeth.

"Hey!" Alec snatches up a cloth, dabbing at a fresh red line on Dante's arm. And I'm trapped, held captive all over again, sharp teeth digging into my lip, my hands tugging uselessly at his hair.

Heat twists low in my belly.

"Ge' off."

Dante smiles, the motion filling my vision. My heart is pounding so hard, I feel dizzy. His tongue darts out, soothing his bite as quick as it came, and then he's sitting back. "Then behave."

"Or what? Will you threaten to shoot me again?"

Alec pauses. The look he sends Dante is murderous. It *drips* disdain. "When did you threaten to shoot her?"

Dante has the grace to look guilty.

"When he took me to pee," I supply, still giddy on this roller coaster. None of this feels real.

The needle stabs in harder this time. *Prod, push, drag.* Dante's jaw flexes, but he doesn't make a squeak. And even though it's ridiculous, I feel bad that I snitched on him. At the time, sure, it scared the crap out of me. But today, after the last few hours, the idea that Dante would actually hurt me feels so clearly bullshit. Even now, his strong hands are bracketing my thighs, holding me gently in place on his lap.

I haven't forgotten how he got that bullet wound: carrying me to the truck.

"Pussycat," I murmur, and Dante's expression is scathing. But he doesn't stop me when I lean in.

His lips are soft. Pillowy. His breath mists warm over my cheeks, his grip tightening on my thighs. The prod and drag of the needle fades away, all sounds lost except the steady draw of Dante's breath and the silky slide of his palms against my legs.

The heat builds in my core. Grows slick and pulsing, and I can't help the whimper that escapes my throat as we grip and sway together. Dante growls, low and rumbling, then his hands leave my thighs to cup my face, to tilt my head, to let his tongue thrust into my mouth.

Dante kisses like a mobster. He takes what he's owed.

It sends ripples down my spine.

And what the hell am I doing? Have I lost my last thread of sense? Reality rushes back in, cold and clammy, and I lurch backward off Dante's lap, cursing loudly as I step on my bad ankle. He stares at me, eyes hard and pupils blown wide.

"Roxy—" Alec reaches for me, tries to steady my elbow, but I hop out of his reach, too.

This is fucked. It's all so messed up.

"I need a shower." I was just giving an excuse, but now that I say it, it's true. I desperately need scalding water and scented steam. I need to wash the blood and sweat and dirt off me. I need to *think* straight, for one freaking minute. "Don't come in."

"Don't flatter yourself," Dante snarls, but I ignore him. Alec, too. And the room spins a little as I limp across the stained carpet.

The bathroom door wedges shut when I shove it with my shoulder. My ragged breaths bounce off the tiles. And I sink down onto the toilet and bury my face in my hands.

* * *

What kind of a person kisses her captive? Not under duress;

70

not as some kind of escape plan. Because she *wants* to. Because she doesn't like knowing he's in pain, and because she feels like she'll explode if she doesn't.

I'll tell you what kind of person: a basket case.

"Therapy," I grumble to myself, running a bar of soap up my arm. "Freaking years of therapy."

The motel bathroom is about as glorious as the rest of the accommodation. The sink is cracked and listing to one side; the mirror is clouded with age and flecked with god-knows-what. The shower is a rusted metal head over a beige bathtub that I'm pretty sure used to be white.

Doesn't matter. The water's hot and it keeps coming. That's all I'm asking for right now. And besides—I'd been hiking for days already before I fell off that ledge. I stink worse than the motel.

I've been in plenty of dive hotels over the last few years. Running a travel blog on a budget, you'll see some stuff. Cockroaches. Bare wires. Snakes under the bed. My tolerance for crappy accommodation is *high.*

An ex-mafia prince and a dingy bathtub? Not such a big deal.

It's weird. Being in that bedroom with the curtains drawn, it was like a pocket outside of time. But here, with daylight filtering through the frosted glass window, I remember it's early afternoon. That most people are outside, enjoying the sunshine.

I could probably join them. What are the chances that Angelo guy would care? That he'd even remember what I look like? I could limp out there, clean under my dirty, bloody clothes, and blend with the crowd. Find a local cop, or hell—just pretend this fever dream never happened and finish my freaking vacation.

I'm not going to do it. Leave them just yet.

71

I won't think about why.

"Kidnapping assholes," I remind myself sternly. "They're kidnapping assholes."

Assholes with big, bleeding hearts.

Guilt pinches in my chest, and I shampoo my hair, scrubbing a bit harder than necessary. I shouldn't have done that. Played them off each other that way. Shouldn't have kissed Dante like I needed the air in his lungs, all while Alec sat there, his jaw clenched tight enough to shatter.

I owe them nothing. And yet my stomach curdles at the thought of his blank, distant eyes.

The shower head sputters, spraying suddenly icy cold, and I slap off the water before it freezes my skin. It's an ordeal, hopping around and trying to dry myself with the threadbare motel towel, but I don't call for help. Gotta keep *some* dignity. And when I finally push back out into the bedroom, my crusty clothes pinched in one hand and my towel tucked tight under my arm pits, there's a men's flannel robe laid out on the single bed.

"Alec got it at the front desk," Dante says, sounding bored. He's propped against the double bed headboard, his legs crossed at the ankle, and he's going for casual but he's holding his arm too stiffly. It's hurting him, then. "He's gone out for supplies."

"Like clothes?" I limp to the bed, tossing my shorts and sweatshirt onto the carpet. My towel slips as I pull the robe up and over my arms, but Dante doesn't look. He stares at his thumbnail, like it's the most fascinating thing in the world.

"Maybe." He shrugs. "Whatever he thinks we need."

It must be nice to have that kind of trust in someone. To surrender completely to their judgment. I've been on my own now for so long, my parents nothing more than a yearly holiday

72

card, that it seems exotic. An alien culture.

"Well, I need clothes."

"Demanding, aren't you?"

"Is it safe out there?" I talk over him. "For Alec. Will he be okay?"

Dante rolls his eyes, still staring at his fingernails. "I don't know, Roxy. Let me consult my crystal ball."

I huff. "You're an ass."

He looks at me at last, raising his eyes while his head is still bent. "Yes. I am."

The lifted arm is an invitation. A peace offering, of sorts. I've got my own bed, there's even a rickety chair in one corner, but I'm a sucker because I go to him. Limp across the carpet and crawl up onto the bed, wincing at the movement in my ankle.

"Yes." Dante urges me up to the headboard. Arranges me against his side, his good arm draped over my shoulders. "Come up here, bella. Welcome to the sick bay."

"How's your arm?"

"Bloody. Stitched up. Incredibly manly."

I snort. "I'll say."

We don't talk about the kiss. Nor the man hunting us, or the hard flints of hurt in Alec's eyes when I left for the shower. We sigh and lie draped over each other, exhaustion sinking deep into our bones.

"This bed is excruciating," Dante murmurs after a while, half asleep. "I wouldn't make a dog sleep on it."

"Good thing you're not a dog."

His even breathing is the only reply. And a little while later: "I need to shower."

"I used up all the hot water."

Dante sighs, a great, long-suffering gust of air that flutters my hair against my cheek. "Roxy. You vengeful little harpy. Are we even yet?"

"For holding me captive?" He grunts. I hide a smile. "Not quite."

Maybe it's messed up. Maybe it's some Stockholm Syndrome nonsense, but the tragic fact is that I haven't felt this *held* for as long as I can remember. Even when they had me tied up, they took care of me. And now, when they've seen the error of their kidnapping ways, when they're going all-out to *protect* me...

It's powerful. A heady rush.

"Do you think I need therapy?"

The laugh rumbles from deep in Dante's chest. I want to rest my cheek on his ribcage and feel it reverberate.

"Everyone needs therapy. Even boring people who don't get kidnapped."

"Alec doesn't need therapy."

Dante snorts. "He needs it more than anyone."

I lie there for a minute and think about that. Pull the statement apart and look at it from all angles. And there's something there, something he's telling me, but whatever Dante's complaints, this bed is pretty damn comfy. Too comfy to think straight. My eyelids grow heavy, my breathing slows, and I roll slightly, tucking tighter into Dante's side.

"Sleep, bella," he murmurs into my hair. His fingers play through the strands.

And I do.

12

Alec

The town is nervous. A frazzled energy hangs in the air, buzzing like flies. I stride across the square and focus on that.

That, and not Dante and Roxy. Alone together in the motel. Moaning into each other's mouths, tugging at each other's clothes. Were they waiting for me to leave the whole time?

My footsteps drum against the paving stones, and I shove my hands deeper in my pockets. The mountain breeze is fresh, laced with pine and lake water, and I breathe deeply, but the knot in my chest doesn't ease.

It doesn't matter. We're running for our lives; this doesn't *matter*.

I walk faster, eating up the sidewalk with angry strides. The trees bristle with drying leaves, turning gold for the fall, and the mountains that rise in all directions are capped with snow. Lonely Mountain stands the highest, looming over this little town, and everyone who lives here must feel constantly small.

Even though I'm moving openly through the space, I'm still aware. It would be more noticeable to skulk along the edges of buildings—better to cross openly, fearless, and draw fewer eyes. My senses are heightened, straining for any sign of Angelo, the hairs raised on my bared forearms.

I hunted Dante like this once. Prowled after him, so determined to see him behind bars. So determined to make the Marino prince pay for his crimes.

Most of them weren't his. I know that now. Well—the worst crimes, anyway. The violent, depraved ones. Those were his father. And it was those gut-turning crimes that broke Dante's will, that made him cut all ties and flee to the mountains.

I tracked him just like this. Through motels and greasy diners. Through changed name after changed name; over state lines and along freeways. Until finally, I had to choose—my career or following Dante.

I chose Dante.

He was always my weak spot, even then.

We got lucky this morning. Though the bags were left in the cabin, Dante and I both had wallets and phones in our pants pockets. We're not flush with cash, but we've got enough to make do. To survive, so long as we keep Angelo away.

I start with the town pharmacy. Pick up some things to take care of Roxy's leg and Dante's arm—I should have come here first. Too late now. It's too late now for a lot of things. I grab deodorant, toothbrushes and toothpaste too.

Next, I fill a paper grocery bag with snacks. Apples, pre-made sandwiches, chips, juice boxes. Dante will flip, but I don't care. He'll make do.

I get the clothes last. Plain t-shirts and sweatpants for all of us, plus fresh socks and underwear. And all the while, I watch for Angelo out of my peripheral vision, blinking so rarely that my eyes run dry. The check-out guy gives me a funny look, but

I pay without a word, peering over his shoulder at the street outside.

Nothing. No sign of Angelo. That could be good, or it could be very bad. I step back into the crisp sunshine, our supplies tucked under one arm, feeling for the hundredth time how exposed I am out here. How easy it would be for a bullet to punch through my chest.

My footsteps echo as I stroll back to the motel. I take a looping, circuitous route, checking in dusty shop windows to make sure I'm not being tailed. Strains of tinny radio music float out of open shop doors, and for a surreal moment I let myself imagine that this is innocent. That the three of us are really just tourists, here to enjoy the sunshine and fresh air. Maybe to fish or try hiking the mountain.

We couldn't stay in that motel. Not if we wanted Dante to stop complaining. So maybe a nicer hotel, or one of the rental cabins by the lake, with a private rowing boat bobbing at the dock...

Yeah. That's it. That's where I'd take them.

It's such a sweet image, it steals the air from my lungs. Makes a lump grow in my throat. So I cough, once, and push it from my mind. Bring myself back down to earth with a thud.

It's a daydream, and there's no time for that.

I head back to the motel.

* * *

"Anything?" Dante watches from the bed as I peel the curtain an inch away from the window. A street lamp glows orange nearby, muting the stars overhead.

A whole day. A whole day hiding in this motel, holding our

breath as we brace for Angelo.

He hasn't come. And when I scan the motel parking lot, it's as empty as it's been all day.

"Maybe he left town." I let the curtain drop. "That was the plan, right? He'd assume we ran, since that's the smart thing to do."

"We're being dumb on purpose? Like a double bluff?" Roxy wrinkles her nose, her temple resting on Dante's shoulder.

They've been like that since I got back. Glued to each other. Even when one of them gets up to pee, they seal back together afterwards like it's nothing. The most natural thing in the world.

I sit on the edge of the single bed, ignoring the ache in my chest. Guess the sleeping arrangements have changed.

"He's grumpy," Dante murmurs into Roxy's hair. Her mouth twitches, but when she looks at me, she seems worried.

"Come over here." She lifts an arm. I stare at it, nonplussed.

"Do you need help? Do you need to go somewhere?"

Roxy huffs. She and Dante are so alike. "Are you always this clueless?"

"Yes," Dante answers for me.

I sigh. And it's been too many hours without sleep, too much adrenaline coursing through my veins, too much time spent watching *them* curling closer and closer. "Apparently so. I'm going for a walk." I push to my feet.

"Is that wise?" Roxy asks, at the same time as Dante snaps, "Sit down."

God, I want to storm out. Leave them and this mountain and this nightmare behind. But Dante's right—if Angelo's still out there, I might lead him here. And I may be bitter, but I'm not about to risk their safety.

78

"I'll get another room."

"Sit *down.*"

"You clearly want to be alone—"

"For fuck's sake." Dante scrambles upright, lunging across the bed to grab my wrist. One yank and I'm toppling forward, narrowly missing Roxy's bad foot. I catch myself at the last minute, bouncing on the mattress in a chorus of bedsprings.

"*Dante.*"

He shoves backward, making space between them. Drags me into the center of the bed and holds me there slumped between them, a vice grip on my arm.

"Huh." Roxy wriggles on my other side. Curls into me just like she did with Dante, and *Jesus Christ.* She's so warm and soft. I press back against her automatically, a plant shoot seeking the sun. "I get it now. This manhandling never worked for you, Alec?"

"I don't…"

I don't understand. I stare up at the stained motel ceiling, my body rigid on the bed, trying to make sense of the last thirty seconds. Heat seeps into me from either side, and I can smell them both. Feel both their chests rising and falling.

Roxy props up on her elbow. Leans over me to address Dante, her dark hair tickling me through my cheap gray t-shirt.

"You know, you could try a little harder. Dust off an emotion."

"Shut up," Dante snaps. I elbow his side.

"Don't speak to her like that."

"Oh, *now* you can talk?"

"Both of you!" Roxy hisses. "Shut. Up." She draws in a slow breath, still leaning over me, twin spots of anger shining red on cheeks. And when she speaks again, the words are low. Calm. We both lean closer, the bed frame creaking, desperate to hear.

"I've had one mobster take me hostage, and another chase me down a mountain. I know it's not me he wants—" she holds up a palm as Dante opens his mouth "—but I don't care. This has been some messed up shit. And now we're hiding out here, hoping he doesn't find us so we live until morning. Correct?"

I nod.

"Correct," Dante rasps.

"Then we're not going to fight. I won't even give you assholes a hard time for everything you've done. We're going to hold each other and talk and do whatever else we feel like, because there is no freaking way I'm spending my last night alive hearing you two bicker." She bites off, muttering under her breath. Something about *pining idiots*.

There's a long pause. Roxy settles back against the bed, pillowing her head on my shoulder. After a breath, I draw her closer. Tuck her tight against my side. And as we breathe together, the tension slowly drains out of my limbs.

"Whatever else we feel like," Dante murmurs after a while.

"Hm?" My fingers trail through Roxy's hair, scratching at her scalp.

"That's what she said. Isn't it, bella? *Whatever else we feel like.*"

"I... yes."

Dante rolls closer on my other side. He's trying to get to her, obviously, but the added warmth still sears my skin. Crackles over me like nervous energy.

"Whatever do you mean by that, Roxy? Explain."

She huffs. "What do you *think* I mean?"

"I would hate to presume."

I snort. His elbow digs in again. Then he reaches over, his toned arm stretching over my chest, and takes hold of Roxy's wrist. Places her hand on my stomach, flattening his palm over hers, spreading her fingers and interlocking them.

"Show me."

13

Dante

I am tired of Alec's nervous schoolboy act. He is cautious, yes. So painfully considerate. But he's not this shy and uncertain person—I've seen the hard glint he gets sometimes in his eyes.

Alec is a man who knows how to take control.

I want to see it.

Roxy's hand is small under mine, her fingers slender and delicate as they scratch at his shirt. When I hold her gaze, she's eager. Hungry. She's a firecracker, our Roxy, and she wants this as much as I do.

As one, we turn to the man stretched between us.

"Angelo…" Alec's eyes dart to the window. To the thick curtains standing between us and the faded town outside.

"Either he's here or he's not." I slide our joined hands an inch lower, Alec's ridged stomach shuddering as we go. The t-shirts he bought are so thin, the fabric shiny and cheap. I will be glad to tear it off him.

But first…

"Alec," Roxy murmurs. "Do you want this?"

His green eyes track to me. Drawn on an invisible line, like he just can't help it.

Two years, on the mountain together. Years before *that*, tangled together as mobster and agent. So many cold nights and words choked back. Even now, he's lingering on the precipice. Fucking coward.

"Say it," I snarl. "Yes or no."

His mouth firms in a line. I've pissed him off, pushed too far, but when I start to draw my hand away, his own slams down on top of it. Alec holds Roxy and I pinned in place, our fingers spread over the hard planes of his stomach.

"You're an ass, Dante."

I roll my eyes. "We are aware. Yes or no."

Roxy blinks up at him, her chocolate eyes so wide. And it's her Alec turns to, nudging his nose along her hairline.

"Yes," he murmurs, the word pressed into her skin.

I'm moving before my next breath. Crawling along his body, settling on my knees either side of his hips. With a tug on Roxy's hand, she scrambles up in front of me, kneeling over Alec's stomach and facing down at him.

She's perfect. Our beautiful buffer.

And so much more than that, too.

I brush her dark hair over one shoulder. Sink my teeth into the muscle, then ease off, licking where I just bit.

"Holy shit." She's squirming, so fucking responsive. Alec's tanned hands grip her thighs, holding her in place, and she tips her head back against my shoulder.

"Kiss him." I draw my lips up her throat. "See if you can bring the caveman out of him."

"Alec has an inner caveman?" Her arm snakes around my neck. Sharp nails scratch at my scalp, and Jesus Christ, I could purr.

"Oh, yes. He keeps it buried deep, but I believe it's worth the digging."

"Dante." Alec's voice is deep. Rough. Roxy's shiver washes all the way back to me.

She leans forward slowly. Places her hands on his shoulders, her fingers flexing at the substance of him. The way he's so solid, so sculpted, carved from the pale stone of the mountain. Her long hair swings forward, brushing along his t-shirt, and though I can't see from this angle, I know the exact moment that their lips touch.

She inhales sharply. He stills, body rigid, and the room is silent except for pounding hearts and shaking breaths. Then his arms loop up, crushing her down against his chest, and their kiss is urgent. Dark and desperate. I glimpse flashes of tongue; the nip of teeth. And all the while I smooth a palm up and down Roxy's back.

Up and down.

I could get used to this. Playing the conductor. Sitting back and clipping out instructions. But it's cold sat up here by my lonesome, and as I watch them groan and grip each other, it's not only arousal thrumming through my blood.

It's jealousy, too.

"Up." I grab a fistful of Roxy's hair. Tug her, firm but gentle, until she peels away and sits back, chest heaving, her body sealed to mine.

"Getting lonely?" Alec asks, and his gaze is knowing. Viciously pleased.

Oh, I will enjoy this.

"More bored than lonely." Can they hear the lie? It doesn't matter—I move quickly, smoothing a palm around Roxy's waist.

Alec bought us all matching sweatpants. I could have shot him then and there when I saw the ugly, shapeless black material; the tragic sight of us matching in the world's worst clothes. But now I find myself glad for the lack of buttons, as my fingers nudge beneath her waistband.

Smooth skin—uninterrupted.

I still. "Roxy." I press my smirk against her hair. She's gripping my wrist, urging my further while holding me tight. "Did Alec not buy you underwear?"

A pink flush creeps down her neck. "No, he did."

"And a bra?" I trail my other hand up beneath her t-shirt. Follow the silky curves and dips of her body, until my fingertips graze cotton. Some kind of sports bra. "Pity."

Alec sits up, crowding her further back against me. And now we're all upright, all pressed together, and he's close to me too. So fucking near, I can smell the motel soap on his skin.

My hand moves beneath her sweatpants.

"She's beautiful, no?" I hold his gaze as my fingers dip between her legs. Find her slick and warm, her breath catching as I tease the line of her pussy. "The perfect captive."

Alec watches me closely for a moment. Like he's deciding something.

Then: "Perfect," he agrees, and slides his hand down her sweatpants to join me.

"Oh my god." Roxy's forehead tips onto his shoulder. We move together between her legs, our fingers brushing, our eyes fixed on each other. But when Roxy whimpers, we're both torn away. Drawn back to the trembling woman pressed between us.

"Please tell me you have condoms," she gasps.

Alec's mouth twitches. "They didn't seem vital." He shifts his arm, sliding a thick finger inside her. My lip curling, I follow suit. I won't be left behind.

"Bullshit," Roxy moans as we stroke in and out of her. "That's such bullshit." Her hips rock aimlessly. Searching for something—anything. I grind the heel of my palm on her clit.

Alec withdraws his hand, and she just has time to whimper before he tugs the shirt over her head. "Up." The bra goes next over her lifted arms, then he's weighing her pale breasts in his tanned hands.

There's something about that sight. Her creamy flesh and rosebud nipples in his larger hands, all scratched and scarred. I slide another finger inside, my gaze fixed on his hands on her chest.

"Suck one," I grind out. "Bite her." I can't do it from back here. But Alec is done taking my orders. He levels me a look, then ducks his head and licks her. So gently; a flick of the tongue.

"*Shit.*" She buries her face in my throat. As she pants, her warm breath mists my skin. And when Alec pinches her nipples suddenly, rolling them into hard beads, I feel the sudden *whoosh* of her gasp.

"You'll have to forgive Dante, Roxy." He speaks to her so casually, like we're drinking coffees in a courtyard, and the blood thrums faster under my skin. I'm so hard it's painful, so hard my teeth ache. "He doesn't know how to treat a lady."

"Not a lady," Roxy garbles, and my grin is savage as I reach up and palm a breast. I'm rougher than he is, but behind my ribcage, I'm dangerously soft for this woman. Melting into goo.

"Roxy doesn't mind." I tug her sweatpants down to her knees suddenly, delivering a sharp smack to her ass. She moans so loud and long that I can't help the smug smile I give Alec. He glares at me as he takes her hips. Tugs her flush against him.

Hello, caveman.

I fight to keep my face blank as he thrusts up against her, rubbing the hard line of his cock on her mound, only the sweatpants between them. Inside, though, I'm sparking with triumph.

Yes. If I can't have him like this, she will.

"Off." His voice is low. "Get off."

We scramble off his legs. Alec stands, eyes dark as he peels his t-shirt off, then shoves his sweatpants down. We both follow suit, stripping naked in taut silence, too afraid to shatter this new dominant mood that's come over him.

"Dante." I jerk at my name. I'd assumed I'd be watching this. Pressed against the wall, fisting my own cock. So when Alec nods at the bed, no room for argument in his eyes, I climb on and stretch out with my throat tight.

He comes to stand at the foot of the bed. Looks at me openly, greedily, and my cock bobs in the cool motel air. For a crazy moment, I think he's going to climb on top of me. Give me his full weight; let me feel the warmth of his bare skin against mine.

But then he turns to Roxy. "Sit on his face." A smirk tugs his mouth. "It's the only way we'll shut him up."

I've *been* shut up, I'm quiet, but I don't say anything. I don't trust myself to speak. And though a tight kernel of disappointment is lodged in my chest, the second I look at Roxy, hunger roars through me again. My mouth waters.

I pat my chest. "Climb on, bella. Alec wants me quiet. He's clearly threatened."

She scrambles onto the bed, all soft curves and wild hair. But she pauses, kneeling beside my head, and murmurs: "Are you sure?"

I grin, shark like. "Very sure. Give me a taste."

She swings a leg over. The room goes dim.

She's everything I hoped for. Slick and salty, so shameless in the way she rocks and moans. Roxy rubs herself against me without fear, without apology, and I snarl against her flesh. Smack her ass and urge her hips to rock harder. She pauses for a second, shifts her weight, then distantly I hear a ragged groan. The unmistakable sounds of someone sucking a cock.

Good. Yes. I want them both to get off. I plunge my tongue inside her entrance, rubbing my nose on her clit, and my growl is muffled when a hand wraps around my cock.

It's small. Slender.

Fucking Roxy. So perfect.

But then another hand joins, bigger and rougher, with calluses on the palm. This one squeezes me harder, tugs me faster, and I choke out Alec's name as I come with my face pressed into her pussy.

As soon as my ears stop ringing, I bear down on her. I lick and stroke and suck until she's shaking, her thighs twitching on either side of my head.

Alec comes with a sharp gasp. So. Now I know what that sounds like. Roxy flops off me to one side, and cool air rushes over my cheeks.

Alec snorts when he sees me. Flushed and sticky. He strides to the bathroom then comes back, tossing a threadbare towel onto my chest.

"I made a mess of you," Roxy mutters, slumped against the headboard. She's pink and sweaty herself, her hair sticking to her forehead.

"Good." I scrub the towel over my face. Then roll over and draw it gently between her thighs. When I glance up, Roxy watches me, so tender, and I can't breathe.

I toss Alec the towel.

"I'll see if there's any hot water yet." I slide off the bed and cross the room, feeling their eyes on my back.

It was perfect. *She's* perfect. He's always been perfect.

And now we have to let her go.

14

Roxy

We leave the motel before dawn. God knows we've lingered here long enough, boxed up inside these water-stained walls with the musty carpet, but somehow I'm still sad to go.

Something big happened in there. Something I'll never forget. Something wonderful.

I laid awake most of the night, chewing on the inside of my cheek and thinking it over. And over. And over. Wrestling with what sort of person this makes me, and if I'm okay with it, and whether I even care. What it means for all of us. Whether it means anything at all.

Oh, well. We haven't hurt anyone. Only each other. And overall, there's been more pleasure than pain.

"I'm sorry about your camera." Dante leans against the motel wall as Alec locks up. He's freshly scrubbed from the shower, opting to dress in his filthy jeans rather than wear those sweatpants again. The morning light is tinged blue, and it makes him look weary. Plays over the harsh cut of his cheekbones.

"Oh, shit." Honestly, I'd forgotten about it. But he's right—I've lost all my photos from this trip. If I want to write up Lonely Mountain, I'll have to start from scratch, and with a busted ankle and no camera.

My backpack, too. I'm kind of screwed.

"Here." Dante pulls out his wallet. He rummages in a side pouch, pulling out something pea-sized and glittering. A sapphire cuff link.

"Fancy." Oh my god, I'm going to drop it. I'm going to forget and put it through the wash.

"It should set you up for a while. Get your travel blog back on track."

I'm nodding, lips numb. "Thank you."

"Don't put it online," Dante warns. "The cuff link. Don't draw attention. Sell it in person somewhere, even if you get less. Sell it in a different city."

"Okay."

"Use a fake name, too."

"This is a lot of homework."

Dante grins, flashing away from the wall and pulling me into a fierce hug. I bury my nose in his chest, breathing him in.

"Why am I crying?" I sniffle, wiping my snot on his shirt. Serves him right. "Are you sure I'm not insane?"

"Jury's out." Alec steps up to Dante's shoulder. He waits patiently—so unlike last night—then pulls me against his chest too.

I inhale deeply. Commit him to memory. God, what is wrong with me? But the burn in my eyes is real, the hole caving in my chest is real, and when Alec slips his arm around my waist and leads me back towards the town, I sniffle harder.

Would staying on the run be the worst thing in the world?

It's not like I have anyone to go home to. And I could run my travel blog from anywhere. Hell, I could start one specific to Lonely Mountain. There's barely anything written on this area—I could break new ground—

"We're going to miss you," Dante says quietly.

Scattered trucks and camper vans rumble past on the street, their engines hushed as they keep below the speed limit. Like they don't want to break the morning quiet. I peer around for Angelo, but there's nothing. No one.

No more excuses to stay.

We come to a stop outside the Mountain Rescue headquarters. It's a small office, wedged between a coffee shop and an outdoor gear store, and I scowl at the display of fishing rods in the neighboring window. All the shops are dark and silent, but there's a light on inside the headquarters.

"Sure about this?" I'm aiming for jokey, but it comes out sad. "It's not too late to take me captive again."

Alec's smile is so heartbreaking, it's like the ground swoops out from under me. "Now that *would* be a crime."

Dante grunts. "You should have only good things, bella."

It's so rare to hear them agree. And I don't know what to do with it, don't know what to say or where to put my hands. I shove them in my pockets then pull them out again. Tuck my hair behind my ear.

"Wow," I breathe when they both stand there, silent. "This is really sad."

"It is." Dante jerks forward, pulling me into another hug like he can't help it. Alec leans past us to the doorway and rings the bell.

"We'll see you inside." He ducks his head, murmuring, his face close to Dante's. I can feel the other man's heartbeat pick up beneath his shirt. "Make sure that you're safe. Then we'll take off. Lead Angelo far away from you."

"You could stay too—" Dante begins to offer, and I'm glad when Alec cuts him off.

"No. Not happening."

I've never had this kind of camaraderie. The sort of kinship where you stay together—no exceptions. No excuses. And I fall in love with them both a little in this moment. Both on their own, and as a pair. The glimmer of what could have been—a bond between all three of us—shines in the corner of my eye, but then the headquarters door swings open and it's gone.

"Yes?"

We turn together. The man in the doorway is gruff. Bearded. Clad in thick flannel. Everything you'd expect from Mountain Rescue. I blink at him, still reeling, and Dante nudges me forward. I limp toward the stranger, heart in my throat.

"Go on, bella. You tell him everything."

The man's eyes narrow. He peers at Alec and Dante, suspicious, but he holds out a hand and steadies me as I come inside. I grit my teeth on the step, then turn around to say goodbye, but they're already gone. Two broad backs stride away across the town square.

"The hell happened to you?" the man grunts.

I sigh and lean against a noticeboard, the pinned fliers prodding my shoulders.

I don't fully know.

15

Angelo

The Dante I knew was a fighter, not a lover. When we were teenagers, growing up together under the cold gaze of our father, Dante would take girls on dates, wine them and dine them, but barely acknowledge them the next time he saw them. It used to drive me fucking insane—they all liked him so much. He was so handsome, so slick, so sharp. And he brushed them all off like lint from his sleeve.

He doesn't brush this one off so casually. When he turns away and leaves her there in the Mountain Rescue, his face is bleak.

I step back from the roof edge. It's so easy to hide around here. The mountains loom up on all sides, and they make all the people feel so small, so insignificant, that they forget to look up. The match hisses as it strikes, glowing orange as I cup it in my palm. Lighting my cigarette out of the breeze.

It's for Dante. He hates the smell of cigarettes. It reminds him of our father. And I want him to remember it all, every fucking detail about the place he left me. Alone. A young man grieving his big brother.

I shake out the match. Take a deep drag, then puff out a cloud of smoke, watching it melt away with the breeze.

I could follow them. Or stay here with her. Either choice is a gamble. Either way, there's a risk of miscalculation.

He looked wrecked to leave her. But would he come back? Would he put his life on the line for this injured hiker—would he stay for her when he didn't for me?

I have to know. The decision is already made.

I draw my phone from my pocket slowly. If I'd planned this better, if I'd been more of a morning person, I'd have made sure I could watch him while I make this call. I want to read the emotions splashed over his handsome face, but instead I'll have to make do with interpreting his tone.

The phone rings twice. Then the line clicks open, but he doesn't speak.

He knows it's me. Only one person should have his number, and it's the neighbor with the truck. That was another miscalculation—assuming Dante was alone out here. But when the fuck did he get a chance to make friends?

"Hello, big brother." I'm the first to break. It's so typical—Dante waiting me out with his cold silence. Me crumbling and showing my hand. But there's a point to this phone call; it's not just a pissing match. "Did you miss me?"

He doesn't answer. God, why doesn't he answer? It's a simple fucking question. I pinch the bridge of my nose, breathing hard. The roof seems to rock beneath my feet, the sky spinning above as my head swims.

Did he miss me?

Fuck. He's not even going to say.

"Where are you?" Dante asks quietly. He doesn't try to bluff me. Doesn't act like they're states away, living it up. That's something, at least. A little respect.

"Never took you for the romantic type. Remember those girls you used to date? You left a trail of broken hearts all the way through the family territory."

Dante says nothing, but he's breathing hard. It's sloppy, this reaction. He might as well howl at the sky.

"This one is different," I surmise. "Or *you* are."

"Angelo," he grinds out. "If you touch her, I will drag you to hell myself."

I believe him. He's a Marino, after all. We were born with the taste of blood on our tongues. But whatever Dante thinks, I have no interest in his cast-offs. If he truly wanted her, he'd have kept her around.

"Meet me. The town square in ten minutes—I know you're near. We're going to take a little drive back up the mountain, brother. I want to see where you've been living all this time."

I've already seen it, obviously. But I didn't get a chance to go inside. I want him to see me inside his space; want to go through his belongings and sniff the air.

There's a long silence. I grind my teeth. "If you won't show me your cabin, she will."

"I'll be there," he snaps. And, faintly, a voice says: *"We'll* be there."

So much loyalty. I drop my cigarette and crush it beneath my heel.

He doesn't deserve it. Dante doesn't deserve any of this shit—not the girl, nor the friend, nor the quaint fucking cabin.

God, I hate mornings.

16

Roxy

The Mountain Rescue headquarters has way too much plaid. Every surface is faded flannel or bare wood made shiny by hand prints. The grizzled bear of a man who let me in ushers me into a cramped office, with two desks pushed against the wall and a bookcase crammed with old-fashioned paper maps.

There is a mounted fish on the wall above one desk.

Dante would die.

My chest tightens at the thought of him and Alec, but I clear my throat and limp further into the room. There's a squashy armchair by a beat-up coffee table, and that's where the man waves for me to sit.

"You need medical attention?" he grumbles.

I think of the bandages Alec wrapped so carefully around my ankle—the way the swelling's already going down. The diligent way he checked me; dressed all my cuts.

"No."

I flop into the armchair, wrinkling my nose at the musty rush of air. It's quiet. The morning is hushed, like people are sleeping nearby, and I wince at the creaking armchair when I lean forward to scoop up an old travel magazine.

Spoons clink against china in the corner of the room.

The man returns, thrusting out a steaming mug.

"We're out of sugar."

"Okay. Thank you."

The man watches me, eyes troubled, then says: "I'm Caleb. You going to tell me what happened?"

Yes. Yes, obviously. That's the plan, right? Alec and Dante disappear into the sunset, and I make my career with the article of the century. To do that, I'll have to tell people, and why not start with this guy?

If nothing else, I need his help. I've got no supplies, no belongings except Dante's cuff link, and I can't exactly limp up the mountain to rescue my backpack myself.

"Um." My voice cracks. Jeez, why is this so hard? "I fell," I settle on eventually. A partial truth. "A bear startled me, and I sprained my ankle."

The man's grunting, already turning to peer at a map on the wall. A map of Lonely Mountain.

"Whereabouts were you?" he asks, following up with dozens of questions about the bear. Did it seem hungry or injured? Were there other hikers in the area? Did it bite or scratch me in any way? I answer his questions as best I can, and as we talk, my eyes drift to the office window.

They're out there somewhere. In the cold morning light, probably speeding down some highway like Thelma and Louise. I stare out of that window like some tragic war widow, and when the truck draws past on the street outside, I blink hard.

I'm dreaming.

Or hallucinating—that's a head wound thing, right? Maybe

Alec was wrong, maybe I'm concussed, maybe—

The truck rounds the corner of the square, and I get another glimpse of the driver. It's Dante, his face rigid, driving and staring straight ahead. I watch, mouth dry, as the truck turns off the square and heads for the road back up the mountain.

Three figures. There were three shadows in the front seat.

Angelo.

"Oh my god." I lurch to my feet, pointing out the window. "Out there. Call the police."

"What is it?" Caleb stands and crosses to the window, surprisingly agile for such a big guy, already pulling a phone from his back pocket. He cranes his neck, staring at the empty town square.

"It's..." I heave a breath. Think about this for a second. Then whisper, "It's nothing. Sorry."

The Marinos. Dante's name can't get out. They'll hunt him down—if the police don't arrest him first. And what about Alec? He's swept up in this too.

I can't tell. They wouldn't want me to.

But I can't do nothing either.

"I have to go." I snatch up my steaming coffee, taking two giant, scalding gulps. No way am I facing a mobster on zero caffeine. It's not right.

"What?" Caleb looks at me like I'm crazy. His hand twitches for his phone again, but what is he going to do? Perform a citizen's arrest for the crime of being weird? "But your ankle—I thought you lost your backpack?"

"Uh-huh." I limp around the coffee table. "I better go get it."

"That's not a good idea."

I shrug, grabbing the door handle. "Never stopped me before."

He sputters, rounding the furniture toward me, hands raised

like he wants me to see reason. But Dante and Alec are with that psycho right now, and they're headed up the mountain in a truck. Me? I've got no vehicle. I barely have two legs. I need to *go*.

"Thank you, Caleb!" I yell as I stumble back onto the sidewalk. He stares at me through the office window, waving for me to come back inside. I force a wide smile then limp off in a hurry, plans forming and breaking apart in my brain.

Transport. I need transport.

I grit my teeth and turn off the town square.

* * *

"Well if it isn't Miss High-And-Mighty."

The tourist bus idles at the sidewalk, its engine grumbling and its windows fogging against the morning cold. The bristly, red-faced driver lounges in the driving seat, one wrist draped over the steering wheel.

Despite the early morning and the deserted town square, the bus is half full already. The tinted windows are filled with bleary-eyed hikers and sunburned tourists in baseball caps.

I bite back the insults lining up on my tongue, and give him my most dazzling smile.

"Hi! You remember me. That's good."

The driver scoffs. "Is it?" He looks around, grinning, but no one is listening to his banter. They're all slumped in their seats, murmuring to each other. At the back, one man snores.

"Yeah! Of course it is." I push my hair back; let my hip jut out a little. The driver's eyes drop, then raise back to my face. "Listen. I left something important on the mountain. My backpack. It had all my stuff in it, all my clothes, my camera—" I don't have to fake the despair about that "—and I'm screwed without it."

"What about your boyfriends?" The driver reaches down, rattles an ice coffee in a holder. "Can't they get it for you?"

Fine. You know what? Some people just want to know you're miserable. It brings them joy. So I ham it up—I let my lip tremble. Wrap my arms around myself and squeeze.

"They, um. They left me."

"Oh?" The driver grins. So pleased. "Shouldn't have got greedy, should you?"

"You're right." He narrows his eyes at me, so I pull it back a bit. "I mean, how was I to know? But... yeah. You're right."

He sniffs, appeased. And when he waves a hand at the bus, he doesn't ask for the fee. He's the king of the mountain, lording it over me, doing me this huge favor—and that's fine by me.

"Thank you so much," I babble as I shuffle up the steps, gripping the railing tight to save my bad ankle. "You're such a gentleman."

He scoops up his iced coffee and slurps it loudly. "'Bout time you met one."

I titter. "Yeah."

Ass.

I find a seat halfway back—far enough away that I don't have to talk to him. And I stare out of the window until my eyes go dry, until my breath fogs the tinted glass. I know they're not down here anymore, but I still can't help looking. Playing that glimpse of Dante over and over in my head.

This is taking so long. And if they're going where I think—if they're heading back to the cabin—this bus will only take me partway there.

I slide down and rest my cheek against the scratchy headrest. *My boys.*

101

What's Angelo doing to them?

17

Alec

Angelo was never my focus. When I was an agent working the Marino case, I was assigned to Dante, and that's who I stuck with. The other Marinos came up, of course—it was impossible for them not to. But even then, Dante was like the sun. He blinded me to everyone else.

Sitting in a stolen truck beside Dante's little brother... I see the resemblance.

Not that I'd ever tell Dante that. But Angelo has the same wavy dark hair, the same proud chin—even the same designer stubble out here in the mountains. He's dressed in standard hiker clothes, same as Dante, but he also wears them with a kind of revolted defiance.

They're alike. It's unsettling, when Angelo's gun is digging into my ribs.

"Go carefully, brother." Angelo sits back, so relaxed as Dante drives. Our truck purrs up the mountain path, swinging smoothly around each bend. "I have such a delicate trigger finger."

Dante says nothing. He's barely spoken since his brother

103

called. And for the first time in several years, I can't read him. He's retreated behind his walls.

"Is this your bodyguard?" Angelo turns to me with a sneer. "There must be slim pickings out here."

We're both silent. The engine growls as we lurch up a steep section of road, and Angelo huffs.

"Fine. You'll talk eventually, brother."

This man has been such a specter for Dante. The only Marino who refused to believe his faked death. He's been relentless, scouring the globe for his big brother, coming close more than a few times. And yet, now that we're sitting beside him...

I thought he would be taller.

It's a stress response—my lack of panic. I realize that. This is years of FBI training kicking in, my brain reverting to noting the surroundings and the mental state of my companions. But beneath my shirt, my heart is pounding.

The cabin. He's forcing us back to the cabin, but why? Surely if he wanted to kill us or simply to take Dante home, he needn't drag us all the way back up the mountainside. This is a risk—a chance for him to lose control—and yet Angelo needs this.

Why?

"Turn here. Take the back road."

So he knows all the routes to the cabin. That's not good. I clench my jaw, staring out of the smudged window as the truck bounces and lurches beneath us. Every time we're knocked around, our legs and sides jostling, that gun prods a different part of my torso.

It's close range. A powerful gun.

I don't like my chances if it goes off.

"Easy," I murmur to Dante when he starts to drive more wildly, wrenching the truck around corners. He blows out a breath but slows, his movements calming.

Angelo peers at me, blatant interest in his amber eyes.

"What do you want?" Dante grits out at last. Angelo turns away from me, and I suspect that's why Dante finally found his voice. "Why are you here, Angelo?"

Something like hurt flashes across his brother's face. But then the cold, sneering mask settles back in, and he snarls, "Revenge. What else, brother?"

He means it rhetorically, but the question hangs in the air between us. Especially when Angelo jabs me harder with the gun—*me*, not Dante. He's barely pointed it at his brother at all. And his eyes keep darting to the bandages wrapped around Dante's arm, a red spot only now bleeding through the fabric.

Interesting.

The truck lurches between a pockmarked boulder and a listing pine tree. We round the dirt path, Dante's cabin flashing into view between the trees, and I send out silent thanks for the hundredth time that Roxy's not here. That we got her to safety.

Dante wastes no time pulling up to the cabin. He's impatient on a good day, and right now the strain is ticking in his temples.

He wants to get this over with.

"Home, sweet home." Dante shoves the truck door open, not bothering to wait for instruction. I wince, the gun digging deeper between my ribs, but then Angelo leans over me and pushes the passenger side open too.

"Out you hop, Dante's friend."

I don't tell him my name. I'm certain he already knows.

Broken glass crunches under our boots as we stride across the deck. The door hangs open—it's not like we locked up—and there are signs of wildlife when Dante nudges the door open.

Furniture is toppled. Pine needles coat the floorboards. The rug is rucked up at one corner, and there's a mound of something that looks suspiciously like animal bones under the desk.

Roxy's camera sits in pieces beside the computer. A pang ripples through my chest.

"Cozy." Angelo strolls past, nudging my abandoned duffel bag with his boot. He turns and raises an eyebrow at his brother. "Five star accommodations."

Dante shrugs. Says nothing. And this silence is worse than goading; it makes Angelo bristle up, anger flushing his cheeks.

"You left for *this*?" he says again, waving the gun around. "For a damp, stupid cabin on this godforsaken mountain?"

"Not for the cabin." Dante rolls his eyes. He's playing things down, still, but he's inching closer, too. Putting himself between me and that gun. "For the mountain fashion."

Angelo snorts, and for a moment there's this kinship between them. A shared joke; a mutual hatred for flannel. But then Angelo's face shutters, and the moment is gone.

"You shouldn't have left. You shouldn't have left me there." Dante frowns, a sliver of emotion peeking through his mask, but Angelo keeps speaking. "Now I have to remind you about family. About what loyalty means."

My lungs seize as the gun swings back around to me, freezing me in place where I'd been creeping toward the log burner. To the iron poker leaned up on its tip.

"Stop it," Angelo spits. "You cannot stand still? Fine. As you wish." He jerks his gun across the room. "Get on the bed and hold onto the frame."

* * *

106

"I've got deja vu." Dante gives me the ghost of a smile as he ties my wrists to the bed frame. Angelo stands behind him, the gun trained on us both, but he doesn't see the relief in Dante's eyes.

He's happy to do this. The asshole *wants* me out of the picture. If he could, he'd probably have forced me away at gunpoint himself.

"What was that? What did you say?" Angelo comes closer, scowling. "Stop whispering. Or I'll gag him, too."

Dante winks at me, the motion so slight I almost miss it, and it would be funny if panic weren't gnawing at my gut. He's tying me properly, the idiot. Tight enough to hold me here, tight enough that I can't help him, and *god*. If we get through this, we will have some fucking words.

"You're a little too good at that, brother."

It's something Dante would say. For the hundredth time, their similarities knock me off kilter.

"I had some recent practice."

"The girl?"

Dante goes quiet. He won't talk about Roxy. He tightens the last rope, the bed frame rattling when I tug it, then he steps back to stand beside Angelo. They could be twins in the gloom of the cabin. The wind whistles outside on the porch, banging the door against the frame, and I lay stretched out on the lumpy mattress, heart thudding.

"What now?" Dante sounds exhausted already. When was the last time he slept? The last good meal he had? The last time he sat calmly, without fear prickling the back of his mind?

Angelo hums, like he's thinking about it. Taking this moment by moment, and not arranging us to his exact specifications.

"It's nice out. Let's take a walk."

It's just like old times, I think I hear him murmur, then their

107

boot steps echo across the deck and the door swings shut behind them. I glare at the ceiling, my wrists chafing against the ropes as I grit my teeth and try to work them loose.

That asshole. He *tied* me. He really tied me. I growl, yanking the bed frame so hard it bounces off the wall.

My ragged breaths fill the cabin when I finally stop fighting. Just for a second, until my muscles unlock. Twenty minutes could have passed, or ten, or an hour. I don't know. I strain to listen, but there are no voices outside the cabin. Nothing but the moaning wind and whisper of pine needles skittering over the floorboards.

They're gone.

Dante's gone.

18

Dante

"You've lost your leverage." It's so strange to walk beside my brother again, falling into step like no time has passed. It makes something ache deep inside my gut. I missed him. "Tied it to the bed. Now how will you keep me in line?"

"You care that much about your bodyguard?" Angelo asks lightly, but he already knows. Already sees. And it's a strange mercy, that he left Alec in the cabin.

Our father would not have been so kind.

A horrible thought occurs to me then, as our boots crunch over the dirt path. Will he go back? Is he saving Alec for later? Bile rises in my throat, and I dart a glance at his gun.

He disarmed us both, of course. I have nothing on me. But if I took him by surprise, if he thought I was coming willingly—

"Don't bother," Angelo snaps. "You were always a terrible fucking liar, Dante."

"Fine." I come to a halt, mentally digging my feet into the dirt. "What's the plan here, Angelo? Are you going to kill me? Or are you just wasting my fucking time?"

109

For the second time, I catch a flash of hurt. But then he's pushing close, eyes flashing, his gun prodding at my gut.

A stomach wound. That's a bad way to go—we both should know. We've seen enough horrors under my father's rule.

"I'll do whatever I like. Don't you think? *God.*" Angelo gusts out an angry breath. "You're so fucking superior, even now. You were too good to stay, to good to leave the goddamn art alone, too good to be fucking discovered." I blink at him, in a horrible daze as he rants on about my shortcomings.

The paintings. The art dealings.

Fuck. I *am* a fool.

If something happens to Alec—this is truly my fault. I brought this upon him.

I'm to blame.

And it's that cold, trickling realization down my spine that brings me back to the moment. That sharpens my senses and tenses my muscles.

This ends now. Enough pageantry.

Angelo always was such a showman.

"Brother." I catch his wrist and squeeze, grinding the bones. The gun waves between our feet, pointing at the dirt; my boot; Angelo's shin. He jerks back, cheeks flaming, but I hold tight. "I'm tired of this. Are you going to make me kill you?"

"Traitor," Angelo snarls. A fleck of his spit lands on my cheek. I march him back slowly, walking him off the dirt path and between the trees. He may know the paths to my cabin, but I've lived here almost two years. I've walked these mountains every day; I know their secret trails, their moods, their wildlife.

The spots where they swallow up hikers whole.

"Stop it." Angelo jerks at his wrist, but my fingers are digging into his nerves. Cutting off feeling; rendering him useless. His

110

knuckle twitches beside the trigger and a deafening bang tears through the morning quiet.

We pause and look down together. There's a small crater by my foot, and a tiny graze down the edge of my boot.

"Asshole," I say mildly. Then I'm walking him back again.

The trees are shivering. Whispering to each other. Birds cry and gurgle overhead, and tiny claws scrabble against the tree bark. Shrubs whip at our legs as I walk him backwards, backwards.

And my little brother lets me do it.

There's no fight in him. Not truly. And if it were only he and I, this would go differently. I might try to reach him.

But Angelo tied up Alec. Threatened Roxy. I won't gamble their safety. This ends now.

"Our father will know." Angelo trips stepping over a fallen log, and I grab his shirt. Yank him upright. "He'll realize what happened. That I was right and you're still alive. You think he won't hunt you? What then?"

"Then you win," I say simply, and Angelo's face shutters.

He didn't want to win.

He lets me steer him back through the trees, past the boulders, to the ledge high above the river. The water snakes down the mountain far below the ledge, the water churning and milky white.

Did he come all this way so I'd do this for him?

"You could stay," I say suddenly. "Disappear with me here."

His mouth twists. "Your insane little brother? Are you crazy?" Then he's tearing his wrist free and lifting his arm, but it's not me he's pointing at. He levels the gun past my shoulder, his eyes narrowing as he takes aim, and I barely have time to spin on my heel and see her.

111

Roxy. Limping out of the trees, white-faced and leaning heavily on a makeshift walking stick.

"No—"

I see Angelo's finger move out of the corner of my eye. And I don't think. My brain is not part of the equation. This is pure body, pure instinct, as I kick out a leg and slam my boot into Angelo's chest.

I wanted to knock him off kilter. Ruin his aim. But as he stumbles back to the cliff edge, he meets my eye, and he's bitterly triumphant.

The river rushes below, a distant roar, and Roxy's stick thumps hollow on the stone as she limps closer.

"Is he...?"

"Yes." I peer into the waters, searching for a dark head. A reaching hand. Anything. But of course he'll be swept far away by now. Those waters are thunderous.

Roxy blows out a slow breath. I blink and turn to her. I'll do anything but process what just happened.

"Why are you here?"

Her stick glances off my side before I can stop it. She swings it again, whacking my shoulder, and a hollow laugh barks out of me. "I'm saving you, you asshole!"

"Oh." I turn back to the water, warmth and grief warring in my chest. "Good job."

Angelo. My little brother.

He would never have allowed me peace. Would never have let me be. And he would have hurt Alec and Roxy if it meant getting to me—I'm certain of that.

I'm still raw as I stare down at the water. Scraped out and aching.

I didn't mean to do that.

112

"I'm sorry," Roxy whispers. She takes my hand. Her palm is sweaty from the pain. "Where's Alec?"

"Tied up in the cabin."

"Huh." She nudges me. "Silver linings, right?"

I wrap an arm around her shoulders. Tug her close and smell her hair, and get her weight off that bad leg.

Right.

* * *

Alec's eyes widen as I step through the door, Roxy wrapped around my back like a rucksack. She's acting tough, but her thighs are trembling where they grip my waist, and she barely put up a fight when I insisted on carrying her.

She's in pain.

"You asshole." Alec wrenches on the bed frame, and I wince at his mottled purple fingers. His chalky white wrists. He's been fighting so hard to get free, he's nearly cut off all the blood to his hands.

"Stop it." I stride across the cabin, kicking an overturned stool out of my way. Roxy grunts as I drop her on the mattress by Alec's feet, but there's no time for manners. I pick at his ties, cursing under my breath.

"That looks painful. Did Angelo—"

"Oh, not Angelo. No, this is Dante's work."

I half-listen to them murmur to each other, tugging and picking at the ties. But it's no use—he's forced them impossibly tight—and I give up with a snarl and march to the kitchen.

The knife glints as I pull it from the wooden block, even in the gloomy cabin.

"Spooky," Roxy mutters.

113

"It wouldn't have hurt you—" I pause and press my lips together as I slice through a tie "—if you hadn't wriggled around like an imbecile."

"Excuse me for wanting to help you."

Roxy nods at him sagely. "He was ungrateful with me, too."

"I didn't need help," I snap, but the reminder of what happened cools my temper. Leaves me icy and aching again. I cut the rest of the ties in silence.

"He's gone," Alec says finally, and it's not a question.

I nod.

Roxy strokes my arm. "You saved my life."

Even so.

He was my little brother.

They don't speak again until Alec is untied and the three of us sit, dazed, on the mattress.

"Look at us," he mutters. He raises a mangled wrist; nods at Roxy's ankle and my bandaged arm. "We look like earthquake survivors."

"It's these clothes." I pluck at the cheap black t-shirt Alec bought on his supply run. "Anyone would look tragic in these."

Roxy hums. "I prefer you in flannel."

I turn to her slowly, a muscle ticking in my jaw. But she's smirking, and I can't hide my answering smile.

Fuck. We're in pain. My brother is gone. My cabin is wrecked, and unspoken things still choke the air between us.

"Don't go yet." Roxy startles, but she doesn't make a joke. She can hear the quiet desperation in my low tone. "I know we can't force you to stay—" she raises an eyebrow but mercifully says nothing "—but don't go yet. Stay another week. Stay two. Write your travel blog. Please."

"I don't..." Roxy trails off, chewing her lip. She's thinking about it. *Yes.*

"You can stay in my cabin," Alec says quietly. He wants this too, just as badly as I do. He's leaning toward her, this yearning in his green eyes. "No tying-up, I promise."

Roxy smirks down at her lap. Plucks a loose thread on my bedspread.

"Hey, now. Don't make promises you can't keep."

115

19

Angelo

The man finds me sprawled on the river bank, laid out like a feast for passing bears. I watch him approach through cracked eyelids, and even that tiny movement sends sledgehammers pounding at my brain.

My body. My *bones*. I've been pulverized. River water has scoured me inside and out; has beaten every single part of me.

I cough, my ribs searing with pain.

This did not go to plan.

I've never been so fully at someone's mercy before. Unable to move, unable to speak, even to blink. I watch the man as his boots draw level with my face; as he kneels and touches his knuckles to my throat.

My thready pulse leaps at his touch. As if whatever life is left in me is screaming for him. *Help me.*

"Huh." The man shifts his weight, pulling something from his pocket. Distantly, I hear him make a call. Tell the person on the other end of the phone about the guy by the river. The man who's nearly dead.

That's me, I think stupidly, but my tongue is too swollen to speak. I lie there as my freezing, soaked clothes cling to my skin, the mountain breeze chilling me down to my marrow.

The man pushes to his feet with a grunt, towering over me. Blocking out the sun. Then something settles over me—something warm and heavy.

A jacket.

It smells like cedar and rain.

Thank you. That's what I want to say—a phrase that has barely passed my lips since childhood. Marinos don't say thank you, don't show any sign of weakness, but it's too late for that, right? I've never been weaker than I am in this moment. My father would disown me on the spot. He'd kick me back into the rushing water.

"Hold tight," the man rumbles, and his voice is as deep as the mountain caves. I shift on the riverbed, then still as agony tears through me.

I can't see his face. His features are dark, the sun shining behind him and casting him in shadow, but I stare at that dark patch like if I blink I'll die.

A savior.

I've never been saved before.

20

Roxy

"Honestly, stop fussing. You're worse than a grandmother. I'm *fine*." Despite my complaints, I take the mug of coffee eagerly from Alec's hands. I'm propped up in his bed, leaning against the headboard, a new laptop balanced on my knees.

My article is half-written on the screen. *The Bear on Lonely Mountain.*

The bear has taken on an exaggerated role in my account of this trip. I left out the stuff about Dante and Alec. Anything that could cause them trouble. Guess I'm soft.

"How's it coming?" Alec nudges me to shuffle up, then sits on top of the covers next to me. He leans close, reading over my shoulder, and I suck in an eager lungful of his scent.

Woodsmoke and pine trees.

My belly tightens.

It's been a week. A week, and he's barely touched me.

Neither has Dante, even though he's spent more time here than sorting out his own wrecked cabin. He's been sleeping on the sofa, while Alec stretches out on the rug. Never mind that it's a double bed, and I keep offering to share.

Do they not want me like that after all? But then why ask me to stay?

"Listen, Alec..."

The cabin door pushes open. Dante stomps his boots on the deck outside, then ducks through the doorway into the warm glow of the log burner. Over his shoulder, thousands of tiny pinprick stars glitter from an ink black sky.

"What?" Alec murmurs, but I clam up. Sip my coffee as the other man shuts the door and shrugs off his jacket.

I can't ask if they still want me in front of Dante. It'd be like dangling a baby seal above a shark.

"How's the ankle?" Dante calls.

"Still attached."

"Ho ho ho." He strolls closer, his mouth twisted in a smirk. "Such a funny lady." The light from the fire and the small lanterns that ring the cabin cast his skin in a golden glow. It accentuates the harsh cut of his cheekbones; his deep, soulful eyes.

I look at Alec instead, but he's just as bad. So pretty I could cry.

"It's fine, honestly. You should let me walk on it again."

"No," they say together.

I throw up a hand, and slosh coffee on my wrist. "For god's sake! Have you forgotten I hiked up the mountain on it?"

Dante opens his mouth, eyes sparking, but Alec speaks across him, low voice soothing. "Of course not. All the more reason to rest it, Roxy."

"Dante got shot! You haven't tucked him in bed!"

They fall quiet. Too quiet. And suddenly I'm sick of this—always dancing around each other. So many things

119

unspoken; never saying what we really feel. I grab a handful of Alec's gray checked shirt, holding him on the bed, then meet Dante's gaze. Dip my chin at the mattress.

He comes over gamely. Sits in that cocky way that tells me it's *his* choice.

Yeah, whatever.

I take a moment to check him out shamelessly. Dante's in a dark red shirt and faded black jeans, a two day beard dusting his jaw. Beside him, Alec looks scrubbed and wholesome, but we all know that's not true.

And I'm sick of all the pretending.

"Do you still want me?" I blurt. "You know, like before. In the motel. Or are you keeping me here as a friend?" My cheeks heat as I talk, but my voice stays level. I'm proud of that, at least.

Alec clears his throat, shifting awkwardly, but Dante's eyes have drifted shut.

"Ah, Roxy." Dante's mouth tugs up. "Always the brave one. So much braver than us."

I'm not sure that's true. They've both dodged bullets and raced trucks down the mountainside, but I don't argue. In this way, at least, they're both so cautious.

"Well?" I can't believe they haven't answered yet. If I weren't pinned by the bed covers, I'd make a run for the door.

Dante gusts out a sigh, like I'm the most frustrating creature he ever met. His eyes open again, holding me in place. "Of course we want you, bella. Don't play stupid."

"And each other?" He scowls, but I set my jaw. "Say it."

Alec scrubs a hand down his face, but when Dante speaks, he turns to stone, his palm plastered to his nose.

"Yes. Of course I want Alec too." Dante huffs. "You are both incredibly stupid."

It's the worst declaration I've ever heard. "Are you kidding me?" I splutter, but then Alec slides a hand around Dante's neck and they're *kissing*, gripping and swaying on the bed, all teeth and groans and harsh sighs.

"There it is," I whisper, sliding further under the blanket. I sip my coffee, watching the hottest live show I've ever seen.

Alec is on one side of my legs, Dante on the other. They meet above me, clashing like two wild animals on a nature documentary, and I'm so small beneath them, they'd *crush* me if I got in the middle of that—

God, I want to get in the middle of that.

They break apart, panting.

"Fucking finally," Dante rumbles as Alec runs a hand up my thigh. They both turn to me as one, pinning me under their gaze, pupils blown wide, and I squeeze my legs together.

"Oh my god."

Alec huffs a laugh, leaning forward and plucking the mug from my hands. He places it on the bedside stool as Dante tugs the laptop away, saving my article quickly and closing it with a snap.

"Oh my god," I say again as all my props are taken away. As Alec peels the covers off me, tossing them to the bottom of the bed. There's suddenly nowhere to hide, nothing to distract myself with, and I seriously wish I'd worn cuter leggings. These ones have a tiny hole in the crotch—one of the pairs rescued from my retrieved backpack.

"What's wrong, bella?" Dante sits back on the bed. Traces a fingertip up my calf, sending sparks skittering over my whole leg. "Are you all talk after all?"

"No," I croak. "I'm not—I'm—*ah...*"

121

"Give her a chance," Alec murmurs as Dante trails his fingertip across my knee and up my inner thigh. It's so light, a ghost of a touch, and it makes me squirm worse than if he'd tickled me.

"No." Dante reaches the seam of my leggings. A dark smile tugs his mouth as my legs fall open, widening for him automatically. "No, I don't think I will."

He continues his maddening, featherlight trail. Up and down the seam of my leggings, until I'm huffing and rocking my hips up to his hand. I don't even notice Alec crawling up the bed to lie beside me until his warm palm slides over my stomach, up to graze my nipple through my tank top.

Searing hot lips press against my throat.

"Oh my god," I mumble.

"Yes." Dante smirks. "So you've said."

It's so much. Two pairs of hands; two warm, sturdy bodies; two sets of glittering eyes. They each focus one hundred percent of their attention on me, and it steals my breath. Leaves me giddy and overheated.

"Please." I squirm as Dante touches me firmer. Strokes the nub of my clit through my thin, holey leggings. I wait for him to mention my crime against fashion, but he just winks at me then hooks his fingers in my waistband. Peels my leggings down my thighs, down my calves and ankles, and kneels between my legs. He prowls forward, leaning on top of me, crowding me back into the mattress, and *god*, I love him like this.

Vicious and primal and dripping with lust. I want him to break me apart. Then I want Alec's soothing hands, piecing me back together.

"She's ready."

"So eager, look at her."

They speak over my head, like I'm not even here, and that

heats my blood too. Leaves me squirming and breathless. I scrabble for Alec, hooking one arm around his strong neck. He licks a stripe up my throat, and it's so unexpected from him, so base, that I let out a ragged moan.

"Take me. Shit, take each other. Please, let's just do this."

Alec snorts. "Your dirty talk could use a little work." But his eyes are heated when he shifts, looming over me, pushing Dante out of the way. Then his hands are on my ribcage, plucking me off the mattress, and I'm being rearranged. Settled down on top of his hips.

Alec leans back against the headboard, brushing my hair from my eyes, and Dante's heat washes over my back as he crowds in close.

"I had Roxy. Stop stealing the show."

"You both have me," I gasp. And it's true—on so many levels. They both send sparks raging across my skin where they touch me. They both make my blood pump hot and my sex clench.

But they both calm me, too. Settle my nerves and soothe my aching heart.

I don't want to leave them.

Not now. Not ever.

"Hey." I scrabble behind me for Dante's neck. Tug him forward, over my shoulder. "Stop hiding behind me. Kiss him."

"I'm not *hiding*—" Dante's outraged splutter is cut off as Alec surges forward, bringing their mouths together. And this was hot before, but being crushed in the middle of it...

My cheeks heat to a thousand degrees.

Alec's hard beneath me, his cock rubbing against my sex. Dante's length presses against my back. I'm pinned, skewered, and I can hear every hitch in their breath. Every ragged exhale.

"Happy?" Dante grinds out when they break apart, but he's

not fooling anyone. His eyes are luminous, his hands roaming greedily up and down my sides.

It's so easy. Falling into a rhythm together. Pulling off clothes and stealing kisses. Sure—there are a few bumps and fumbles. Dropped condoms. Spluttered laughter. But it's so natural, so right, like we're slotting together. Exactly where we belong. And I'm suddenly so glad that it's Alec facing me, when he slides inside me and moisture brims in my eyes.

He winks—*I won't tell*—and I beam at him. So goofily happy, as he fills me. Makes my head tip back on a gasp.

"Dante," I mumble, my tongue thick and clumsy. I can't think straight, not with Alec so hard and deep inside me, gripping my hips and rolling me over his length. But Dante knows what I need, what I'm trying to tell him, and he trails a fingertip down my spine.

"Are you sure, bella?"

"Oh my god," I wheeze. "Yes. Come on. Do it."

I don't stop rocking my hips. Not when Dante cracks open a bottle behind me, something slick dripping between the cleft of my cheeks. Not when his fingertip circles, rubbing at the pucker of my asshole.

Not even when he slides in, up to one knuckle.

"Holy shit." I drop my forehead onto Alec's shoulder. Rocking harder, my body moving on pure instinct now, my brain completely offline. Dante teases me, gets me ready with such patience, and the whole while Alec smoothes his palm in steady circles on my back.

I've never been held like this.

Cherished.

There's a momentary pause. Then Dante nudges against me too, the broad head of his cock so much bigger than his finger. I groan brokenly, my hips pumping harder, faster, and the pressure is so much I can't breathe—

He slides in.

Just a little way. Then he pauses; lets me adjust.

"Roxy," Alec murmurs. He brushes my hair off my forehead.

I thought it would be overwhelming. Being with both of them at once. And it *is* overwhelming, but not in the way I'd thought. Sure, my body is a whirlwind of sensations, nerves skittering and pleasure thrumming. As Dante thrusts deep, I've never been so full. But the part that really cracks my chest open, that steals my breath—it's their tenderness.

Even when Dante's hand cracks against my ass, it's perfect. The precise sensation I need.

"So perfect," he snarls, like he's pissed off about it. And he leans over my shoulder, stealing another biting kiss from the other man. I join in, too out of my mind for finesse, sucking a bruise onto Alec's clean-shaven throat.

"We'll mark him," Dante rumbles in my ear. "Let everyone know the boy scout is ours."

"He's no boy scout." Alec's grip on my hips is iron. Enough to bruise.

"No?" Dante grabs a fistful of my hair. Tugs my head to the side and licks my throat. "I suppose not."

It's perfect. Rough and tender and wild. A sudden release of pent up feelings. And when I break apart, shuddering and pressed between two chests, when they still and pulse inside me, following after—

For a horrible second, I think that's it. All we'll ever get.

But then Alec pulls out first, sliding out from beneath me and strolling across the cabin. He comes back with a damp cloth as Dante slides out too. And they rearrange me in the bed,

125

curling up on either side, their hands tangling together over my stomach.

Silence falls in the cabin. An owl hoots outside.

Then: "I can't believe you two idiots haven't been doing that for years."

Alec chuckles, but when Dante speaks, he's serious.

"Bella. We were waiting for you."

21

Alec

Two months later

"Is it up?"

I climb the steps to my cabin, a hatchet gripped in one hand and a stack of firewood balanced on one forearm. Dante and Roxy are sprawled on the deck, laid out like emperors on a nest of blankets and cushions.

The mountain breeze ruffles their hair. Scatters crunchy golden leaves over the wooden boards. And my mobster and hiker cuddle closer against the chill, the movement automatic, grinning down at the laptop held between them. The pink evening light coats their skin. Softens them.

"Yes. Now the whole world knows Roxy cannot work a canoe."

She smacks Dante's arm, but she's grinning. "Shut up. The blog has to be honest. I can't pretend to be some worldly perfect traveler, or people will smell the bullshit."

"Let me see." I place the hatchet and firewood down on our

stack, then pluck the laptop from the blankets. The site loads easily as I scroll—we upgraded the internet here as soon as Roxy said she'd stay. There was a strict understanding—no more trading artwork. Only the travel blog.

We don't want there to be any reason she'd leave. She's the best thing that ever happened to us. Our mouthy captive.

"Looks good." I smile at her over the screen. It's a great article—a detailed account of a national park one state over. Her photos are gorgeous, too. Raging rivers and towering stacks of red stone.

I'm unsettled to see my face in a few of them. Dante's lucky—Roxy's always careful to keep him out of view.

"They're going to think we're a couple." I hand the laptop back and nudge Dante with my boot. "Just Roxy and I."

He lurches upright, cursing loudly like I knew he would.

"Fuck that. Fuck you! Roxy is *mine*. So are you. Stupid internet—" he breaks off when he feels Roxy shaking with laughter. He turns to her, eyes sparking. "Oh. I see. Is Alec funny, Roxy? Do you like his little jokes?" She shrieks as he pounces on her, tickling under the blankets.

I watch them for a moment. It's so easy to set them off. And when I turn to carry the laptop into the cabin, they're already kissing.

I'll join in a moment. Better to let Dante stake his claim. He gets so territorial.

The cabin is quiet in comparison. Still and shadowed, but the echoes of old conversations hum between the walls. We could leave any time. There's nothing keeping us on Lonely Mountain. But…

It's not an exile anymore.

It's the place we found each other. The place we are completely free and unjudged; lost to the rest of the world. And the place Dante feels closest to his brother. Even now, he misses Angelo.

Maybe one day we'll go. Move on. But for now...

I toss a log in the wood burner. Better warm up for winter.

* * *

Thanks for reading Their Mountain Captive!

Curious about Roxy's tangle with a canoe? Check out a bonus epilogue with the trio here. Peaceful was never their style...

And for more mountain menage goodness, check out Her Mountain Rescue! Read on for a sneak peek. :)

Teaser: Her Mountain Rescue

Holy shit, it's cold.

And windy.

And *wet*.

Can't a girl catch a damn break?

Coming up onto the mountain in February was a last resort. A desperate measure, when catching glimpses of Ezra and—and *him*—around town every day got to be too much. Every time I saw one of them, it was like a kick to the stomach. I was left gasping for breath; completely winded.

And when they both inevitably turned away from me, their expressions shuttered...

God, it hurt. Even though I deserve all that and worse.

This is the downside of living in a small town. It's not the summer tourists, nor the lack of take-out options. It's *this*: being completely unable to escape my ex boyfriend and his best friend. I can't even complain about it to anyone, because I'm the one who left Ezra.

Never mind that it was the worst day of my life.

So while I never thought a few weeks up on the peaks would be *relaxing*, I figured, hey—at least I'd get some privacy. Somewhere to lick my wounds away from their cool gaze. Somewhere to be sad without reproach. And I got my wish in the form of my coworker Stacey's old cabin.

Draped in cobwebs and falling into disrepair, the cabin is

exactly as gross as she warned me.

"No one's been up there for three seasons," she'd said, twirling the key around her knuckle. "Are you sure?"

"Stacey. You angel. I'm sure."

I'd snatched that rusted key like it was the secret to eternal life. And when I hiked for hours, thighs burning, to reach this tumbledown wreck...

Well, she warned me. And I am determined to make this work. I dropped my backpack in the doorway and didn't even rest my aching feet before scrounging up a broom and chasing out the biggest spiders. Next went the dried leaf litter, blown through a gaping hole in one wall. I swept all that crap out, then set my shoulder against a heavy wooden bookcase and shoved until it covered the hole.

Great builder, I am not. But at least now the wind doesn't blow *directly* into my face where I'm huddled on the dusty bed, swaddled in every blanket I could find.

"This is perfect." My teeth chatter as I mutter to myself—clearly a sign that I'm going mad. "The perfect place to nurse a broken heart."

There *is* a romantic sort of poetry to the cabin. Though it's fallen into disrepair, it has the skeleton of a gorgeous old building. All the furniture is solid and well made—maybe even hand carved by one of Stacey's relations—and the fire crackling merrily in the log burner washes everything with a soft glow. The bookcase is laden with old classics and cowboy books, and I even found a stack of faded comics under the wooden table.

It has potential. It's *pre*-cozy.

That's what I'm telling myself, anyway.

A sudden gust of wind slams against the side of the cabin, rattling a row of mugs on their shelf and sending sawdust showering down from the ceiling. I watch, open mouthed, as the heavy bookcase rocks on its base, pushed solely by the wind, several paperbacks dropping onto the floorboards.

"Oh my god."

I lunge to my feet, blankets still clutched around my shoulders like a cape. The wind howls louder, louder than the wolves I pretended I didn't hear last night, and the bookcase rocks so far, I think for *sure* it's going to fall. Books drop onto the floorboards in a steady, thumping drip, and finally my brain comes back online and urges my feet to move.

My blankets slip off my shoulders, pooling forgotten on the faded rug as I grit my teeth and drag the heavy wooden table jerking over the floorboards. It's heavy, dragging on my arm sockets, and when I finally wedge it up against the bookcase, my cheeks are warm and I'm sweating under my goosebumps.

The wind howls.

The bookcase rocks.

The table stands steady.

"Good." I pat the gnarled wooden surface, polished by dozens of hands over the years. "That works. Thank you."

My blankets crackle with fragments of dried leaves as I scoop them up. I shake them out, nose wrinkled against the dust, then wrap them quickly around my shoulders again before flopping back onto the bed.

It's just some wind. A bit of bad weather.

Nothing to worry about.

* * *

My mom taught me a trick when I was a little girl and our heat went out one winter. First, she bundled me up in blankets.

Tucked a hot water bottle by my feet. I mean, she's not an idiot.

But then, she told me to close my eyes and think about the warmest place I could imagine. Back then, it was a tropical island, with coconut trees and white sands and a pirate ship bobbing in the distance. And Mom said to picture it all: the warmth of sunshine on my skin, the baking hot breeze, the sensation of being too hot in my clothes.

I opened my eyes, and I was *thirsty*. Got cold again after a while, but it was nice while it lasted.

Bundled up in my icy cabin, I figure I'll try anything to thaw out my frozen feet. They're chunky with three thick layers of socks, and I still can't feel my toes as I crawl inside my sleeping bag, piled high with blankets on the narrow bed.

I flop onto my back. Blink up at the ceiling, with narrow strips of evening sky visible through the holey roof.

"Alright. *Warm.* Warm thoughts, Bianca."

The tropical island isn't gonna cut it.

Casting my mind back over the last few years, the hottest day I can remember was a day spent climbing with Ezra. It was high summer, unusually hot for Lonely Mountain, and we were exposed to the sun in a valley. Ezra was stripped to the waist—he likes to climb shirtless, the show-off—and his muscled chest and toned arms were seriously distracting. He kept catching me staring, and he was so thrilled every time, laughing and prodding my ribs.

He was just as bad, though. Especially when I drew my long brown hair up into a ponytail. His gaze snagged on the curve of my neck; on the hollow of my collarbone. And when he took me to the rock face, dusting our hands with chalk and showing me how to tie onto the rope, he kept finding excuses to touch me.

He stood behind me, linking our fingers together before showing me different holds on the rock.

He checked the buckles of my harness. Stole a quick inhale of my neck.

That was an early date. So early, we were still shy around each other. Unsure but so excited.

I screw my eyes shut harder, tears spilling into my hair.

Yeah. That valley with Ezra. That's the warmest memory I have.

The cliff sides funneled the sunshine down to us, catching us in a heat sink. And it got so hot, we both burned, and I *never* burn. Every breath was warm and dry as it passed through my throat, and my top stuck to my skin by the time we were done climbing. Ezra shot up that wall like a mountain goat, while I puffed and struggled my way to the first ledge.

I shift in my sleeping bag, the bed creaking under my weight. Maybe it's in my head, or maybe it's the blankets, but I feel a little better. Part thawed, even as my chest aches. When I wriggle my toes, I think maybe I can feel the thick wool of my socks.

Clearing my throat, I try to hold onto that memory again. The laughter; the shy glances. The shiver of insects in the long grass. But, inevitably, my brain tracks away from Ezra to another man. This is a well-worn pathway in my head, worn smooth like a riverbed after I've followed it so many times.

I'm weak. But it's impossible to picture warmth without thinking about Caleb Olsen.

Maybe it's the copper strands in his hair, or his gentle chuckle. Maybe it's those soft flannel shirts he always wears—so criminally cozy that all I want to do is bury my nose in the center of his chest and inhale. It would be different than Ezra's chest.

134

Caleb is bulky where Ezra is wiry; padded where Ezra is rock hard.

I huff loudly, burying deeper into my sleeping bag.

Even here, I can't escape them.

But... as my hands roam idly under the covers, brushing over my stomach, something else heats my blood. I came up here to forget them, yes, but this is an emergency, right? Survival of the thirstiest. And my body responds to this far more than my little mind games, heat crackling through my frozen limbs. My cheeks burn where they meet the icy air above the lip of my sleeping bag, and I bite my lip as I let my hands wander.

Lower... lower...

My fingertips dip inside my leggings.

There's no excuse for this. For the thoughts that have haunted my waking hours since I first met Caleb at the cookout. My only saving grace is that Ezra is always there too in my daydreams, when I let my mind truly go free. Touching me. Kissing *him*. And then Caleb's big hands span my waist and *squeeze*.

I whimper.

Thank god there's no one here to see this. The locals in town know me as a practical young woman. Endlessly pragmatic; never showing undue emotion. I rule the lakeside summer camp with the strictness of a school matron.

Now I'm dipping my fingers between my legs, tears streaming into my hair as I think about the two men I can't have.

Crash.

The sound of shattering glass jolts me upright, my legs trapped in my narrow sleeping bag. My pile of blankets slides sideways onto the floor, and I stare across the cabin, my heart slamming in my chest.

Broken glass litters the floorboards, glinting in the glow cast

135

by the log burner.

And punched through the shattered window, a tree branch stretches towards me across the room.

I blink. Wait with held breath for the cabin to collapse with me in it. Count backwards from one hundred, mind racing. What is there to do? I can't fix the window—not right now.

I flop back onto the bed with a groan. Shivering again.

This goddamn wind.

* * *

Check out Her Mountain Rescue here!

136

About the Author

Kayla Wren is a British author who writes steamy New Adult romance. She loves Reverse Harem, Enemies-to-Lovers, and Forbidden Love tropes.

Kayla writes prickly men with hearts of gold, secretly-sexy geeks, and—best of all—she's ALWAYS had a thing for the villains.

You can connect with me on:
- https://www.kaylawrenauthor.com
- https://www.bookbub.com/authors/kayla-wren
- https://www.amazon.com/~/e/B08CL281V1

Subscribe to my newsletter:
- https://www.kaylawrenauthor.com/newsletter

Also by Kayla Wren

Year of the Harem Collection:
Lords of Summer
Autumn Tricksters
Knights of Winter
Spring Kings

Standalone titles:
The Naughty List
Roomies

The Office Hours trilogy:
Extra Credit
Bonus Study
After Class